WHEN THE TIME IS WRIGHT

A CHRISTMAS NOVELLA

RENÉE A. MOSES

GUSSYFLO PUBLISHING

Copyright © 2021 by Renee A. Moses

Original cover photo by Алсу Вершинина on Unsplash

ISBN: 978-1-956798-11-1

GussyFlo Publishing

For Gustavia & Misty
You two are together now. As much as I hate it, I trust that you
are in a better place. Holidays aren't the same with you both. I
love you so much.
We will see each other again one day.

FOREWORD

Hey peeps! So before you get into When the Time is Wright, I want to make sure I do right by you. This book is about a woman who was divorced by a man due to the lack of fertility.

If this is a triggering subject for you, you may want to skip it. I do believe Tanji's story to be healing but it's not every woman's story. I go in detail of her emotions, misconceptions, and view of herself because of her loss. I also give her what I feel is needed to feel whole again.

If you have experienced what she has, I pray that God's hands cover you. I pray that the right options are brought to you so that you can be the mother you know that you are. Even when our bodies don't cooperate, I trust that God will fulfill what he has revealed to us. If you want to be a mom, you already are. It's just a matter of how. Trust it, meditate on it, and move on it. You got this!

Love Renée

CHAPTER ONE

"Un-fucking-believable!" I scrolled down my ex-husband's IG page after my girl Shanice had texted me to do so.

"Un-fuck what?" Momma asked from behind me.

I spun around in my desk chair. "Nothing! You didn't hear a thing."

"Oh, but I did." She placed a basket of clothes on my bed. "You left these in the dryer."

"I was gonna get those." I met her in the middle of the room near my bed. "You folded them too? I told you not to do that."

"Girl, hush. Now who fucking who?" she asked again. I burst out laughing at her curiosity.

I rolled my eyes, realizing I'd have to show her what I'd just seen, eventually. I handed her my phone. "Awww! Whose cutie pie is this?" she inquired about a baby boy lying on a blue blanket with a circle around the number nine. I swiped to the left for her to see the remaining family photos. "Now, hold up now! That's—"

"Yep."

My ex-husband of only one year had a nine-month-old son. Nine fucking months old!

The recognizable woman with him in the pictures had carried his child well before my marriage had ended. Our divorce had only taken maybe four months at the most. All of which we'd lived in the same house.

Antonio never mentioned being with anyone else. Let alone getting anyone pregnant. Then again, that had Antonio written all over it. He had no etiquette with anything serious. Some guy served me the divorce papers at the house we shared. I had no idea Antonio had even filed. We'd talked very little in the end.

"That bastard done knocked some woman up? Wait..." Mom stared at the ceiling, counting on her fingers. "You mean to tell me he'd been screwing around while you were married?"

"Looks like it." The jerking at my heart persisted, but I kept it together. I didn't want my momma to catch wind of how much this bothered me. I'd claimed to have been over him already. "Thank you for the laundry, Ma. Next time, let me know if I leave my clothes. I will get them and fold them myself."

"Child, please. You are my baby. You have enough on your plate. More so, mentally and emotionally. Trying to get yourself together with starting over, the craziness with your apartment, and your business. It's a lot, Tanji Bear. I can fold a few things to help lighten your obviously heavy load. It reminds me of when you were younger. Except you were on the other side of the argument then. You used to use the basket as your closet."

Ugh, speaking of my apartment. One of the freaking maintenance guys had planted cameras in the units of single women. The only reason anyone found out was because a neighbor's boyfriend had tried to fix her thermostat after maintenance was taking too long. He'd discovered four hidden cameras in her apartment.

Word got out as we learned her unit was one of many. A lot of leases were broken, including mine. My dad had searched my place and came up empty, but neither of us felt comfortable with me staying there any longer.

"Yeah, well, I'm grown now and I like to do my laundry." Momma let out a soft breath. I appreciated her wanting to help; however, my dirty clothes were my responsibility. "Anyway. Do you need help with dinner?"

"No. I'm going to the store in about an hour to pick up some things. Wanna come?"

"Sure."

An affectionate smile landed on my mother's face. Her eyes glossed over before she plunged at me with wide-open arms. "I'm so glad you are home, Tanji. I missed you so much."

I matched her embrace. "I've missed you too. I will get out of your hair soon. I'm narrowing down my choices."

She let me go. "You should get the condo downtown. I can come visit you and we can run the town together." Momma strutted across the room, waving at imaginary people.

"I just might since it's my top choice."

"Good. I will leave you to it. I'm gonna go call your dad to see if he needs anything."

I smacked my lips because she always prompted him with the same question only to get one answer. "You know he's gonna say he needs you."

"Ahhh, yes he will. It never gets old."

"Yeah, it does," I mumbled.

"Smart ass." She left, closing the door behind her.

The moment I was alone, a jolt traveled through my body. Antonio had a baby? All those years of trying, we'd come up

3

empty-handed. I didn't want to cry. Especially not over his ass. It made no difference to the tears wetting my face.

How was any of this fair? He had dumped me since I couldn't have children and this asshole got one out of someone else. I was the problem. It confirmed my feelings of being the defective model wife that Antonio had quickly replaced.

Seven years of marriage down the drain after wasting our lives together. Throughout it all, we'd experienced four miscarriages and failed fertility treatments. Our heartbreaks and losses had the potential to break the strongest of marriages down. I only hoped we could've been stronger than most. I was wrong.

Realizing that all of our setbacks truly fell on my shoulders hurt more than anything. My marriage had dissolved because my body refused to produce children. Nothing else mattered to Antonio more than passing down his family name. Since I'd failed to hold up my end of the bargain and give him children, he made the decision not to hold on to me.

I texted Shanice back, confirming I'd now seen the baby. She called me to check if I was okay. We talked for an hour about how much I wasn't. Shanice couldn't change my mind about all this being my fault. My self-bashing session would've lasted longer if Momma wasn't ready to go to the store.

Now, I needed a half-gallon of Cookies Over Texas ice cream from H-E-B. Once I emptied its contents, I prayed I'd be over this recent information.

CHAPTER TWO

"THANK YOU, SON! I CAN'T GET AROUND LIKE I USED to." My mother greeted me with a side hug from the passenger seat of my car.

I rolled my eyes on the inside, knowing better than to let her see it. Then she'd be upside my head. This lady was milking her recent injury for sure.

"No problem, Mom. Where do you need me to take you first?" This was my Friday off. She kept tabs on me enough to catch me at the most opportune times.

My mother didn't hover over me too much. She had a life. My dad thoroughly enjoyed chilling at home with the remote in his hand these days. Mom liked to get out and do whatever she could to keep herself busy.

As we got older, she'd always remind us that once my baby sister moved out; she was going to party until her dying day. Apparently, we'd stolen her younger years and this was her time to catch up.

My sisters and I joined her for some of her activities. Others she did alone—like the line dancing class that now had a boot on her foot. She'd twisted it while learning a two-step.

Mom must've been going hard on the dance floor because most of the people in her class were fifty and up. The instructor usually took things slow enough to avoid any injuries.

By week three, they had done something that had my mother calling us like her damn foot had fallen off. It was a simple sprain, so she'd be wearing the boot for a couple more weeks. It'd definitely come off before Christmas.

Five minutes into the first stop, Mom hopped on my back about settling down. My parents never used to push until I'd turned thirty-four three weeks ago. Now, the topic inched its way into every conversation.

I wasn't opposed to the idea. Hell, I actually wanted it more than I let on. However, you needed a woman to have a wife, and wifey hadn't made her appearance in my life yet. So, I'd dabble with females who didn't want the same things as I did. At least until wifey showed up.

Mom and I turned the corner from the bread aisle in H-E-B and saw a woman leaning over the front of a basket. "Damn, she got a fat ass!" My mouth reacted before I could stop it.

Mom clicked her tongue. "That's why you ain't gonna find love. Always worried about the wrong thing."

The woman ahead of us spoke in a voice I swore I recognized. "Momma, Daddy just asked for some beer," she said. Seconds later, another woman came into view.

"Well, look at that!" Mom limped her way over and spoke to Ms. Octavia. So, that meant that the other woman was...

"Tavier?! Oh, my gosh! Hey!" Tanji Baily's smile might have been the cause of all the glaciers melting. It warmed every inch of me. Every single inch.

I froze for a beat because I could not believe it was her. Plus, looking how she was looking. Tanji reached out and wrapped her arms around me after she hugged my mom.

"Tiny Tanji? Aww hell naw. What you been eatin'? Booty

enhancing chips?" I grabbed her arms and spun her around for another blessing to my eyes.

"Shut yo' ignant ass up. Damn, you still get on my nerves." She lifted her eyes to the ceiling with her hands resting on her hips.

I raised my hands to apologize. "I'm sorry. I just...You weren't this sexy when you left." Her head leaned to the side. "I mean, you was fine, but you ain't have all that."

"You are such a pervert. How about you focus on my face?"

"That's the only familiar thing about you, though. I need to get acquainted to the new member of yo' body." I sucked in air through my teeth as I took one more peek. "If I'd known you'd fill out like this, I would've taken my shot before you got married. Shit, you'd be knocked up every year prancing around me with all that."

"Hmph. First of all, grow the hell up. Second, it's not that big." Tanji turned her head toward her back to check for herself, proving my point.

"If you can look at yo' own ass, it's that big."

"Wow! How can you still be the same after all these years? Not an ounce of class. Just say whatever pops in that filthy head of yours."

"Man, I don't even get this riled up. I saw that thang and immediately was about to pounce and get yo' number. I didn't realize it was you." She rolled her eyes before looking toward our mothers, still talking about whatever. "Nah, you remember back in high school when dudes would be like, 'Wool, woop! Pull over.' They ain't never did that shit to you and you know it."

"Damn, Tavier. You act like I had nothing at all. I wasn't no long back chick. I was slim." She punched me in the chest. "Is there anything else you can say about me? It's been almost ten years since the last time I saw you."

I sucked my teeth. "That's because you got married and dropped all of us common folk. Took his last name and he took you away. Over in St. Louis, acting like you forgot how to use a phone."

"Boy, please. We wouldn't talk on the phone if I did call. You're too busy gawking at females' booties and all."

I chuckled and nodded. "This is true. However, my sisters would've gladly taken the call." Tanji dropped her head slightly. "I didn't mean to—"

"It's cool. I was in my bag a bit and Antonio didn't make it any better. I allowed him to keep my isolated up there. My only friends were the wives of his friends and a few people I worked with. Anyone from home didn't make the cut. I kinda had my reasons not to reach out, but that's on me."

"Hmm." I crossed my arms as we followed our moms, who slowly led the way through the aisles. "So, where's Mr. Tanji anyway?"

"Shit, somewhere living his new life with his new baby."

The tone in her voice chipped at me a bit. I'd always given her a hard time back in the day, but I didn't want to see her hurt. I halted in the middle of the aisle and grabbed her left hand to check out her ring finger. It was empty. "Yo, are you serious? When did that happen?"

Tanji shrugged before pushing the basket. "Like a year ago."

"Damn, T. I didn't know. You'd think my nosy ass sisters would've warned a brutha. Unless they're in the dark too."

"They're aware. I moved back here not too long ago. We hashed out everything and are cool now."

"Oh, that's some bullshit. Nobody told me you were here."

"Well, surprise! I moved back to Screwston for good."

"That's what's up. So, let me get yo' number so we can hang out and hash some things out. I got some bones to pick with you myself. One in particular." I dropped my eyes to my jeans and she followed suit.

"Eww!" Another hit to the chest. "You are really a mess. You are not my type, playboy."

"Shiiiit. I'm every woman's type who wants their back cracked with no strings attached."

"I cannot with you." She giggled as she left me behind and joined the women at the end of the cleaning supplies aisle. My mother's basket was half full by the time we'd checked out. I hadn't noticed her picking up anything. All because of Tanji 2.0.

Tanji had always been a gorgeous girl with a heart of diamonds. Pure and sweet. She hung out at our house just as much as my little sister hung at hers. All three of my sisters were close with her, though. Tanji became part of our family by default since our moms were best friends.

We all went to the same schools, mostly at the same time. I was two years older, but I was only ahead of her and my youngest sister by one year in school because of my November birthday.

I couldn't believe that fool had let her go. No matter the situation between them, only a fool would drop a dime like Tanji. Little booty or the donk she possessed now; she was a catch for any man. If I played my cards right, I might have to get in the game and take her off the market for good.

CHAPTER THREE

"I saw how that boy was looking at you," Momma interrupted my daze about the same boy she spoke of.

Tavier had always had the girls' attention in school, and I was sure that hadn't changed. However, he'd never had mine as well. That boy really was like family and family didn't think of each other in the ways my mind had traveled in the last five minutes.

All our joking aside, he could get it if he were from a different bloodline. I wasn't looking for anything besides temporary remedies for the boiling pot between my legs. Miss Thang missed being touched by someone other than me and the few toys I used. Since moving back, she had only tasted one guy. He'd done okay but she wanted Tavier to be next.

Tavier's height hadn't changed, but he'd put on a few in the best way possible. He looked like he'd easily break a man's neck with his grip. Better yet, he looked like it'd take no effort to throw me up in the air effortlessly, catch me, then guide me onto his dick.

Speaking of his dick. Even in loose jeans, it had Miss

Thang purring for a simple touch, nibble, brush up against, or anything with it.

"Momma, ain't nobody worried about him," I completely fibbed.

"Now you know damn well you can't lie to me. You like him too. Whatever happens, be careful. We are too close to all of them to get caught up in any drama if y'all get involved."

"Momma!"

"What? I'm telling the truth." She pointed her finger at me from the passenger seat. "At least we wouldn't worry about in-laws being stupid like your last ones. That bitch was a deep down to the core type of bitch. Can't nothing help her."

"You have a point there."

My ex mother-in-law wasn't a fan of my family. It was more because she obsessed over her son. He was her prized possession, which made me somehow belong to her too. The woman didn't want to share me with anyone.

I had reminded that woman frequently that I wasn't an orphan when I'd met her son. I had a family that loved me and would be a part of my life as much as she was. I didn't miss her at all.

"Ooh, you and Tavier would make some pretty babies." Her smile took her wherever those babies were in her imagination.

"With the way things are playing out, babies may not be in the cards for me. So, yeah."

"Aww, Tanji Bear. Don't say that."

"It's okay. Really, Momma."

She smacked her lips. "No, it's not. Especially after that no-good trifling negro put you through hell and cheated on you to top it off."

I shrugged for lack of anything better. "Technically, by the time he'd messed with her, we had already drifted apart."

"Mmm. Who's the other woman? You seen her before?"

I drew in a breath and held on to it for what felt like forever. A quick nod, and just like that, my eyes released streams down my face. "A coworker of his."

"Oh, my baby." She rested her hand on my thigh and squeezed it. "Fuck them."

My mouth flew open. "Momma!"

"No, I'm serious. Fuck the both of them. How dare he? I hope they both get hit by a car."

"Lord!"

Momma bobbed her head with closed eyes as if she was willing it to happen. "Yep, let them get hit, but only he dies. She can live since the baby will need her. They can go straight to hell for all I care. Motherfuck both of them."

"You are a mess, Ma."

"Messing with my baby." She hit the car door. "Ooh, I'm mad, girl. Why you had to tell me that? Let me catch his bitch ass momma in these streets. I'ma tell her bitch ass about her bitch ass son. Mmmhmm. They can go to hell and live a bitch-ass eternity together."

My tears still flowed, but for a good reason this time. I couldn't stop laughing. Momma was dead ass. I hoped we didn't encounter anyone related to my ex-husband because she'd let them have it and then tell them to send the message to Antonio.

"I need a drink. Let's go drink." Momma looked at her watch. "We'll put the groceries up and go to Pappasito's. You still love that place, right?"

"Heck, yeah. Let's do it."

MY OLD FRIEND HAD THE NIGHT off, so we'd planned to catch up over drinks. She was a bartender by night and a teacher by day. Bartending was only part-time since it had gotten her through college. She loved the atmosphere and had refused to let it go once she'd snagged her teaching position.

As usual, Lilah was late. I'd called her twice since I'd gotten here. Sitting at the bar on a Thursday night by myself wasn't the worst, but it definitely pissed me off. I hated being stood up. At least have the decency to make the other person aware that the plans changed. A simple ask.

Ten minutes later, I picked up my phone one last time to reach her. When she didn't answer, I cussed her out in a to-the-point text.

On my way out the door, a group of guys damn near trampled me. I kept my head down so none of them would say anything. This weight gain had gotten me a lot of unwanted attention lately. By the time I came across the last guy, I heard him say my name. Without stopping, I lifted my head and spotted Tavier. I continued on my way after giving him a nod.

"Hold on, T. Where you going?" He caught up with me.

"Home, Tavier." There was that damn purring again.

Miss Thang couldn't relax around him. With this cold air blowing about, my body heated just looking at him.

Tavier took my hand. "Come hang with me."

"Uh, no! You here with all them dudes. I'll pass."

He swiped his hand toward the restaurant. "Man, they don't need me. I wanna chill with you. See what you been up to."

"I can answer that right now and save you the trouble. I've been minding my damn business," I said, trying the hardest not to laugh.

"All you gotta say is you like me too, T. We grown."

"Ha! You're funny. Ain't nobody thinking about you."

"I've been thinking about you."

CHAPTER FOUR

Tanji tried to play hard while her eyes disagreed with the words that spewed from her lips. "Boy, what do you want with me?"

"Why do I gotta want something? We friends, right?"

"Since when?"

"You mad at me or something? 'Cause all I'm tryna do is chill with you."

"Tavier please, you don't need to spend no kind of time with me. I'm used goods just depreciating as we speak." Her hands dropped at her sides.

I fell back a couple steps, palming my chest. "Tell me you're joking. You don't mean that shit, T."

She shrugged and turned away from me. What the fuck did that nigga do to her?

"Now you have to have a drink with me. We gotta get all the bullshit out of your mind."

Tanji shook her head but stood in place. "I'm gonna go." Her eyes glossed up as if she'd cry if she blinked hard enough.

"Hell no. I'm serious." I held both of her hands and lifted them to my chest to pull her in closer. "I don't want to hear you say no shit like that ever again. Do you hear me?"

She dropped her head. I lifted it and leaned down to her eye level. "Tanji, I'm not fucking playing with you. We like to go back and forth and shit, but that right there...We not doing that shit. I don't give a fuck what that nigga said or did to you, I better not ever hear that shit come out of your mouth again." I searched her eyes until she understood I meant every damn word.

"Okay, okay! Can I go now?" She rolled her eyes like a teenager in trouble. "I don't want to go back in there."

"You don't have to. Come with me." I still held one of her hands and led the way to my car.

"I drove here."

"Is your car locked?"

"Yeah."

"Then it'll still be there when we get back." I texted my boys and told them I was leaving. After vaguely answering why, we got in my car and took off.

At the first stoplight, she broke the silence. "Tavier, where are you taking me?"

"You'll see when we get there."

Like I'd hoped, she didn't fight me on it. Tanji settled into her seat and sang under her breath to my playlist. My vibe was chill, which matched my music preference. The entire ride went smoothly. Once I pulled into my garage, she finally perked up a bit.

"Wait, you live here?"

"Yeah, why?"

She snickered and slow clapped. "God, why are you playing with me like this?"

"What are you talking about?"

"How about I literally put down my deposit this morning to move in these damn condos next month."

I chuckled. "Yo, you for real?"

"As real as this ass you can't keep your eyes off of."

"Aww, shit! We about to be neighbors!" Then it hit me that our moms were damn near sisters. "Aww, shit. We about to be neighbors."

Tanji squinted her eyes at me. "Okay, what was that second one about?"

"Man, my people don't know where I stay."

She dipped her chin. "What do you mean they don't know where you stay?"

"It means exactly that."

"What are you? Batman or some shit? Why is it a secret?"

"Moms be poppin' up and I hated that shit. So, the last time I moved; I didn't tell them where."

"Well, your secret it safe with me."

"My girl." I gave her a pound before we exited my car. I led her to the elevator and pressed the eighteenth-floor button. Tanji cackled like a crazy person. "What now, goofy?"

She tilted her head to the side. "Take a wild guess."

"Aww, hell naw. This your floor too?"

"Tavier, what's going on? This is insane. I'm not even gonna say what unit. I can't jinx it."

"Man, it's already done. Ain't like the units will change if you don't say it out loud." We made it to mine and she leaned on the wall across from my door.

"Um, this might be harder to hide. I'm moving right in there." She pointed toward my neighbor's door.

That couple had gotten married last year and now the wife was pregnant. I'd had a couple conversations with the guy at the gym downstairs. They were moving into a house next month.

"What are the odds? You might as well move in with me."

Tanji giggled and followed me inside my apartment. "Right?" She spun around in the kitchen. "Ooh, I cannot wait to get into my place. It's so nice in here. Well, minus the all black everything."

"Don't hate on my fly. Black goes with everything."

She got comfortable on a barstool at the small island. "Yeah, but it's so dark. You need some type of color, Tavier."

"The walls are white. That's enough." I grabbed two bottles of water to start us off. She opened hers immediately.

"You need a woman to spruce it up. You might need to stop hiding from your family and let them help you."

"Or you could help." I winked.

Tanji took a gulp of water. "Or your girlfriend. I'm not about to decorate your place."

"You can be that too."

She side-eyed me, then elevated her brow like I'd insulted her. "Be what exactly?"

"Stop playing dumb. You feel this thing between us. Don't lie."

"Ha! What thing? Disgust? Annoyance at your stupidity?"

I rested against the fridge. "So, you gonna make me work for it, huh?"

"Boy, if you don't shut that shit up. What do you have to eat? I need a drink too."

"I'ma get you, Tanji. Especially when you move in. I'ma have you falling in love and shit. Watch."

"All we're gonna watch is a damn movie. Now stop playing and feed me."

"I got something I can feed you." I tugged on my belt.

She laughed with her hand covering her mouth. "I cannot deal with your crazy butt."

My kitchen stayed stocked with liquor. I had nothing for us to eat, but that was the reason I'd settled in this area. Restaurants were within walking distance.

"Let's take a little stroll down the block. We can find some

17

food and talk about that bullshit you said about yourself earlier."

Tanji rolled her eyes and dropped her head back. "Do we have to?"

"Hell, yeah. You are too damn smart and sexy to think some shit like that about yourself. And don't even front like you were joking. I know you meant it. Now, I'm taking it upon myself to help you unlearn all the dumb shit your ex put in your head. Then when I'm done, I'ma put something else in you."

She dropped her head back for a belly laugh. I loved witnessing that part of her. Seeing her, even a little upset, set a fire under me to make sure she had less and less of those moments and more of these.

"Something is wrong with you. I am not going there with you. I ain't one of your little hoes. Plus, we are too close to being family."

"Shiiiit. There ain't one piece of DNA of ours that matches. That is the exact definition of we can do whatever the fuck we want. Besides, when I'm done with you, you gon' have my last name. Bet money."

"Nigga, how much? I could use a vacation."

"A'ight. Keep talking. I'ma have you eating them words."

"Whatever, Tavier. Let's go so I can eat something for real."

Tanji Wright. That had a good ring to it. She could think I was playing for now, but too much was going my way. God was setting us up for real. I felt that to my core.

CHAPTER FIVE

My homeboy came over to kick it after work. He lived three blocks from my building and was the one who had suggested I moved out this way. The environment sold it for me. Good food on every corner. Not the stuff you could get anywhere either.

Our wings had arrived ten minutes ago. Stephan devoured half of his twelve wings and some of his fries. His sliders hadn't been touched yet. For someone so little, he had a crazy appetite We stood the same height at six-two, but he was lanky as hell.

Unfortunately, I told that fool everything. We were like brothers, which meant no filter.

"Why is this one different? You literally fuck any female who isn't related to you."

"Nah, man. A brutha got standards. She had to be fine and single."

"Oh, yeah. No paper bag broads and no claimed ones. I remember." He chuckled, wagging his finger in the air. "Bruh, you really not gonna get at her, though?"

I'd tried my hardest to keep Tanji off my mind. Steph with

all these damn questions wasn't helping. "Look, she reiterated we're too much like family." I shrugged it off, hoping to end the topic.

Tanji had chilled with me two nights ago and nobody but her ass lived in my thoughts since. I'd almost had her. Stephan didn't know that part of the story. All he knew was I'd left him and the guys for her.

While Tanji was over, we'd ended up watching *Almost Christmas*. Mo'Nique was a damn fool in that movie. I loved how Tanji dropped her head all the way back to fill my apartment with her loud ass laugh. It made me laugh harder. I wanted to hear it all the time.

After one too many drinks, our conversation switched to past sexual experiences. Somewhere in between, Tanji straddled me on the couch. I kept my mouth shut so she felt free to do whatever was on her spirit. Who was I to stop her?

Once her shirt had come off, I dragged slow kisses on the exposed parts of her breasts. Maybe I got too comfortable or some shit because as soon as I bit that same spot, she shook her head and looked at me sideways. It looked like she had suddenly recognized me. Two seconds later, she demanded I take her to her car.

"So was my sister. That didn't stop you."

My head fell forward into my palm. "Steph, dawg, you gotta let it go. It happened one time and neither of us even remembered the night. The morning after was the only indicator that something had went down."

"She's still my sister."

"Man, she may be your sister, but she's also a woman. One who chose ya boy." I popped my collar. "You can't stay mad, though. It'll never happen again."

"Yeah, whatever." He took a swig of his beer. "What y'all doing for Christmas? I might swing through. Pops' new lady can't operate a microwave, let alone boil water."

We laughed after admitting the woman was fine than a motherfucker. She didn't need to cook. Stephan's pops picked her for all the right reasons for him. People got too hung up on certain skills women didn't pick up or couldn't master. That old man stayed with his grill locked on cheesing. Ol' girl was doing something right.

I MET MY SISTER AT MEMORIAL CITY MALL SINCE she worked nearby. She had some last-minute shopping to do and I had all of mine to knock out. If it didn't get checked off the list today, they'd get a gift card.

"You know I could've just bought the gifts and dropped them off at your place," Fatima suggested once we hit the first store.

"Not happening."

"Tavier, it makes no sense that we can't know where you live."

I shrugged. "It also makes no sense that my mother walked in on me with a woman six different times, Fatima. Six." I held my fingers up in her face until she shoved them away. "I fell for it for the first two apartments. This time is a no-go. I need my privacy and she was not one to respect it."

"Okay, but I never popped up on you though. Never would."

"I believe you, Tima. However, Rhonda Wright would find a way to get the key from you or at least get the address out of you. Y'all are straight up punks with Mom."

Fatima pursed her lips and nodded with no more push-back. "I guess. Oooh, this is cute!" She picked up a sweater and rested it on her swollen belly. "I could rock this."

"Yeah, maybe after you drop the load you're carrying.

That shit ain't gonna work with all this." I made circular motions near my baking nephew.

The gender reveal had been one for the books. All the women boohooed for half an hour straight. Fatima and my brother-in-law, Richard, already had three girls. Both swore up and down that no matter what, this was the last child. When the balloon popped, and blue confetti fell out, you'd have thought the Texans had finally won the Super Bowl.

By the fifth store, I'd gotten my other sisters and all five of my nieces a couple of gifts each. We were in line to purchase some cologne and a watch for my dad, plus an expensive ass purse for my mom. I'd heard of the Michael Kors brand but never paid attention to all the handbags and whatnot. Fatima swore our mother would love it.

My sisters left the more expensive gifts to me since I didn't have dependents yet. At least that was how they explained it. My little sister, Brianna, got suckered into the same thing, but since she was planning a wedding, I had to hand over the wallet alone.

"Aight, I'm done. I done spent a whole G, messin' with yo' ass."

Fatima chortled while I struggled to carry the bags and avoid bumping them into other people. Since she had a natural load to carry, I held her bags too. Dodging through the crowd, I thought I saw a familiar face. A few moments later, we were face-to-face with her.

CHAPTER SIX

 Tanji

"Tanji! Hey, girly!" Fatima greeted me with a side hug to avoid her belly.

Tavier's orbs consumed me. My skin's temperature hiked as I fought like hell not to stare back at him. A rushed glance his way, I said, "Hey."

"What's up?" came out of his mouth and I instantly felt stripped. My sight dropped to everyone's shoes as I reminded myself to breathe.

Who gave him permission to be so damn fine? Who gave me permission to view him that way?

Obviously, avoiding him completely was out of the question. Our families were too close. I did, however, expect to only run into him at his mother's house. The city was big enough for us to stay out of each other's way. As of the other night at his place, that was my goal.

I hoped I wouldn't make this weird, but the awkwardness stemmed both ways. We stood for what seemed like eternity, with no word from any of us. Fatima tilted her head. "Oh, that's it? I thought y'all had more to say."

"Why you think that?" I snapped, assuming he'd told her

what happened. Paranoid was more like it. We came close to making a mistake I'd prefer to keep it between us.

Fatima narrowed her eyes. "Beeeecause y'all always talk crap to each other." She gently elbowed me with a smirk on her face. "What's wrong with you?"

I swiped my hand, praying to get out of this. "Nothing, girl. I'm tripping."

"Yeah, you are." Fatima backhanded Tavier in the chest. "Why are you so quiet?" she asked Tavier.

"I talk when I have shit to say."

"Exactly. Anytime you and Tanji are in the same room, all you do is run your mouth."

"Man, we standing in the middle of a mall. We don't have to do that shit here. I'm sure she got stuff to do." His eyes darted straight to my breasts when he looked my way, taking my mind back to the other night. I crossed my arms over my chest before anyone clocked my nipples poking through this damn sweater. My swollen areolas tried to rat me out.

"What's wrong with y'all? I'd swear you two saw each other naked or something." Fatima laughed at herself alone. The moment passed for either of us to shut that notion down. "Oh, my god! Did you...? Did y'all screw each other?"

"No, Fatima! Your brother is weird." I kept my regard on her. "So, how are the girls? I'll be over for Christmas. I want to buy them something. What do they like?"

Lord knows I only wanted her to talk to keep us off-topic. I had no intention of buying her kids anything but candy. Now, I'd have to make another trip to Walmart. I noted the brands the girls were into while Tavier burned a new hole in my ass. He only had one thing on his mind. It ran through mine too. If I messed with anyone, it couldn't be someone I'd run into often. He was officially off-limits.

Something tickled Fatima and had Tavier and me looking at her sideways. "Sorry, y'all. This boy is kicking up a storm.

You wanna feel?" she asked me. It was sweet of her, but I declined. "Tanji, it's really okay if you touch my belly. You're basically my little sister. I don't understand why you think it's rude. I'm the one asking."

Fatima and I had caught up a bit over the months I'd been back, but I hadn't been totally honest with her or her sisters. Keeping my miscarriages from them initially was to protect me from all the sympathy stares and hopeful conversations. They'd mean well, but it wasn't something I'd wanted to talk about. All I had told them was that my ex-husband didn't care for me to keep in contact with anyone back home.

Part of what I explained had truth in it with a sprinkle of fabrication. He'd once told me I needed to call them and find out what they were doing right, so I'd figure out what I had done wrong. It made me resent my family all because they lived their lives as they should. My jealousy took hold of me, so I completely shut them out.

Whenever I learned of my pregnancies, no one outside of my parents, Antonio, and Shanice found out. They were the only ones I had time to tell before the baby was no more. Momma understood my request for privacy because, after the first loss, nothing felt real. I didn't allow myself to get excited and wouldn't dare share my news with the world until I had someone to show for it. Expecting disappointment made it hurt a tad less when it came true. Each time, I had gotten exactly what I'd expected. No baby.

Fatima and Cheyenne conceived and had their babies while I kept losing mine. No matter what I did. It wasn't like they had anything to do with the reason my pregnancies failed. However, seeing them with their kids and expecting again made me keep a reasonable amount of distance.

"I know, girl. But umm...let me go. I gotta help my momma bake all them pies for the church's bake sale," I told them. It wasn't a lie since we planned that for tomorrow.

"Okay, boo. I'll talk to you later," Fatima said with a half-hearted smile.

"Love you," I told her before heading on my way.

Tavier was on my heels. "Aye, wait up." We stopped near a kiosk. Before the woman opened her mouth, I told her we weren't interested in whatever she wanted to sell.

"What do you want, Tavier? I have to go."

"T, I don't want shit to be crazy between us because of the other night."

I nodded. "Okay, it won't."

"It already seems like it."

"It's not, Tavier." The more I spoke, the more he countered. Miss Thang cared the least about what he said. The sound of his voice coming out of those full brown lips only made me want to bite them.

"You keep telling yourself that. What's up with you then? You acting like your puppy just died." Tavier set his bags down on the ground between us.

"What are you doing? Fatima is waiting on you." My eyes darted to where we'd stood earlier. No Fatima.

"Man, she doing her third round at the food court for samples." We used to do that all the time back in the day.

Tavier opened his arms, motioning his hands for me to come closer. "Boy, no." I swatted his hands away. Unfortunately, his long arms reached me and pulled me into him, anyway.

"Your ass look like you need a hug. Don't fight me with yo' mean ass. Just let me hold you for a minute." I did as he said and let him. The bags on the floor blocked us from getting all the way close, but it was enough for me to sink into his big ass arms and take a whiff of his cologne. I didn't want him to let me go.

"Uh-uhn." Fatima walked up on us. "Something is going on with y'all."

I tried to pull away, but Tavier held onto me. "Mind yo' damn business. It's just a hug."

"Mmmhmm. Next time it'll be with no clothes. Tanji, don't fall for it. He's charmed his way into too many pairs of panties. I met them females and you are so much better than them. Don't let him trick you."

"Damn, Tima. I can't comfort a friend?"

"Friend my ass. Don't do it, girl." Fatima shook her head at me.

Tavier kissed my temple only to tease her. "You good? Don't mind her. She mad 'cause she could never be friends with a man without fucking him."

"One of those friends is now my husband. At least I can keep 'em. Girl, his longest relationship lasted less than a year and it ended months ago this late in his life. Can't keep a woman if someone paid him to. I wonder why."

Tavier rubbed the back of his head like he was in the hot seat. "'Cause I haven't found the one I need."

"Negro, please. You've found plenty. They just don't want to settle with a hoe."

"Chill, dummy. You don't know whatchu talking about." He looked at me while he picked up the bags. "I'ma see you soon, T."

I waved while taking steps in the opposite direction. "Yeah, okay. Bye."

"What? I don't get an 'I love you'?"

I chuckled. "Boy, bye." He got on my damn nerves. He also turned on the faucet between my legs. Miss Thang drooled any time we were in his presence. She wanted the trouble.

The other night, her ass had taken over entirely. After eating and watching a movie, his smiles lingered, and his voice dragged in a way that put me in a trance. I couldn't remember how we'd started talking about the craziest places we'd had sex.

All logic flew out of the window as Miss Thang took control. Whenever my brain had any liquid influence, she thought she could do what she wanted.

The sensation of that man's teeth dragging across my skin had woken my ass up. Tavier got added to the untouchable list. I didn't really think of him as a brother, yet the familiarity might as well label him as such.

Being grown and recently single, he appeared in a different light. I had to dim that immediately and permanently. Like Momma said, if we took it there and it ended ugly, things would change between all of us. I'd rather not take that route. I valued our somewhat of a friendship more.

CHAPTER SEVEN

 Tavier

I LEFT MY PLACE TOO LATE. EVERYBODY AND THEIR momma was out on the road. Stephan made it to my parents' thirty minutes before I did. He was basically part of our family. They expected him for the holidays about as much as they expected me to show up.

The first thing that caught my eye when I walked through the front door was this nigga all in Tanji's face in the living room. The girly grin she wore had me heated. What the fuck were they talking about? Why did she look too damn happy talking to him?

"Finally!" Cheyenne hollered on her way to me. "We waited on you to play games. Everybody already ate. Oh, it looks like your boy might sweep T off her feet. He's been on her ass ever since he got here." She hugged me. "I'm assuming you didn't tell him she's already taken. At least in your head." She laughed as she poked my temple.

Cheyenne was the epitome of a big sister. She looked out for us and caught things that others didn't see. Lying to her was useless. My brief encounter with Tanji at the mall with Fatima had popped up in my sisters' messy conversations.

Chy came to me privately and straight-up asked me what happened. I punked out, telling her everything except specific details. I admitted that I wanted Tanji in the worst way.

"Little brother, you better do something. She over there looking real comfortable."

"Fuck," I said under my breath. "Good looking out. I'll handle it."

My parents sat with Tanji's parents, talking about politics and conspiracy theories as usual. I listened to their conversation only for a minute before interrupting them for hugs.

"Hey, baby. You want me to make you a plate?"

Before I opened my mouth, my dad spoke for me. "No, Rhonda. That's a grown man. He can make his own plate."

"You're a grown man and I make yours."

"Oop!" Ms. Octavia let out and turned away from us as if she wanted to stay out of it. She giggled after mouthing something to Mr. Mason.

My dad pointed at me but kept his eyes on my mom. "Well, if his ass would stop screwing anything in a skirt, he'd have a wife to make it for him. You need to stop babying him. That's why he thinks he don't need a wife. He got you taking care of him like—"

"Terrell Wright, you sure you wanna fight this fight?"

My dad glanced around, and after finding eyes on him from all directions, he threw his hands up. "Okay. But you know I'm right."

"I can make my food, Mom," I told her.

"I'll get it, baby. Especially after your father did all of that."

"Stubborn ass," Dad said.

"And you love to kiss it," Mom countered.

"Aww, naw. Come on, now." I covered my eyes when Mom looked like she was about to do something I didn't want to see.

"Boy, shut up and come get this food." She led me to the kitchen and piled on some of everything. The night before Christmas, we usually had something deep-fried. Mom fried catfish, soft-shell crab, and shrimp. Plus, she cooked greens, mashed potatoes, and corn on the cob. Nobody cared about eating healthy during the holidays.

I spoke to everyone before sitting with my soon-to-be brother-in-law, Dorian, and my brother-in-law, Richard. Tanji barely nodded when I dapped Steph up. I did it hard enough for him to understand something was up. He looked at me crazy before sitting back down next to Tanji. All that fucking giggling and shit had me on edge.

My in-laws kept me occupied long enough to fill my belly, though not enough to keep me from ear hustling. I didn't hear much with The Temptations playing in the background and my mom singing along all loud. She jammed the same playlist every year. After I finished, I asked to talk with Stephan outside.

No sooner did the front door shut that I went in. "Nigga, what the fuck you doing?"

He shrugged like he couldn't tell what was up. "Whatchu talking about?"

"Man, you all up in her face like I ain't tell you what I'm tryna do."

"Whatchu mean? I thought you weren't gonna get at her. You said she didn't want to because y'all were like family. I remember that shit clearly, T."

"Yo, fall back, bruh. For real."

"If you don't want her, why can't a brutha slide in? I deserve a good one too. From what I've seen so far, you sleeping on a gem. When I see something, I—"

"Dawg, don't even finish that shit. It's gon' be fucked up if things go my way. You can't even have those thoughts about her. Dead whatever bullshit you thinking about. That's me."

"Do she know that?"

"Yo, Steph, I'm not playing with you."

"Damn, nigga. A'ight." He lifted his index finger from his cup. "Next time, keep it a hundred. You out here frontin' and shit. Got us out here arguing over a girl like some damn kids."

I laughed, realizing how childish I sounded. I still didn't give a damn. Even if Tanji didn't end up with me, she was not about to fuck with one of my boys. Hell naw.

CHAPTER EIGHT

Tavier and Stephan acted strange when they came back inside the house. Stephan barely said two words directly to me. I didn't care either way. He was only a distraction from having to converse with Cheyenne and Fatima. The both of them looking at me funny had me paranoid. This was a prime example of why I couldn't mess with Tavier.

"Hey, sexy," Tavier whispered to me from behind. I rolled my eyes to mask the flutters which usually caused me to blush.

I turned his way. "Hi." Then I turned back around. Tavier joined me on the couch. "Can we talk for a minute?"

I shook my head. "Nope. Not unless your name is Tevin Campbell."

He gave a half-suppressed laugh before groaning. "Tanji? Come on. Only a few minutes."

The way his sisters watched us hinted that he had told them something I hadn't. "I said no, Tavier." I kept my attention on my phone, playing a word scramble game—my go-to stress reliever.

He placed his hand on my knee. "Please, T? I won't take much of your time. I promise."

"Ugh, fine." I got up and let him lead the way to the front door.

"Where y'all going?" Cheyenne asked all loud, leading everyone's attention our way.

"We're going somewhere to mind our damn business. A place you've never been and probably never will. Acting like a damn self-employed private eye," Tavier answered his sister as loud as her inquiry. She scowled at him for two seconds, then laughed with everyone else after her husband agreed with Tavier.

"We'll be right back," I assured her because they were ready to play the games. Hell, I was too.

"Okay, but if y'all take too long, we're starting without y'all," Cheyenne warned us.

Tavier opened the door for me. I stopped at the porch, but he took my hand and headed toward the sidewalk. "Hold up. Where are we going?"

"Just down the street."

"We can't have everybody waiting for your ass to take a damn stroll, Tavier."

"Then I'll get to the point. Come on." Two houses down, he finally opened his mouth. "Why you in there cheesing all in my boy's face?"

"Oh, hell no. Is that what you brought me out here for? If so, let me take my ass back in the house." I turned around, intending to leave him by himself.

"Tanji, I'm not tryna sound immature. I only want to know if you're interested in him because I thought we were having our little thing."

"What little thing, Tavier? We only kissed once."

"Shiiit. That was a helluva lot more than one kiss. I still feel your skin under my fingertips." A chill rushed up my spine. He traced his finger on the back of my hand. "The texture of your soft skin still lingers on my tongue." He blew out a slow breath. "I'd have more to say if you hadn't freaked out on me the other night."

"Tavier, we can't go there."

"Why? It only shows you feel the same way I do. What's stopping us from doing what we both want?"

We walked past a house with the biggest damn inflatable I'd witnessed up close. It was taller than the house. I bumped his arm with my shoulder. "We are kinda friends. Our families are extremely close. I don't want to jeopardize anything."

"What if we actually are what the other needs?"

"Here's the thing, Tavier. I can't get into another relationship. I can't give you a future."

Tavier stopped me with his hand on my belly. I held his hand there and closed my eyes. The thought of no one ever growing inside of me right where he placed his hand flooded my mind.

We stood in silence at the corner of the street. Lights were glaring from every angle. These people took their Christmas displays seriously. I pushed his hand off of me when I opened my eyes to him studying me. "Why you keep saying sad-sounding bullshit? Is it just some poor excuse or do you really believe it?"

My mouth opened to answer, but he put his finger in my face. "Tell me the truth, Tanji."

I rolled my eyes. Tavier knew me well enough to recognize whenever I lied. "The reason I don't have a husband right now is because I can't have kids. So when I say I can't give you a future, I mean it literally."

Tavier chuckled, then smiled unfairly. Nothing about this was funny to me. "Is that why you keep saying those things?"

"It's the truth."

"Man, shut that shit up. You are not only worth what you can give. With or without kids, having you in my life is the only thing on my mind lately."

"Having me in your mind is not the same as having me in real life, Tavier. It sounds cute now, however, when you're itching to pass your name down, I can't give that to you."

"Who gives a fuck? I'm telling you right here, right now I want you. We can raise a damn dog together for all I care. I'll name that motherfucker Wright and call it a life."

I couldn't help but smile. Feeling wanted still made my cheeks warm. "You're sweet, but I'm sure you don't know what you're saying. All this right here," I said, motioning at my body. "It has you temporarily distracted. It'll wear off and you'll face the same reality Antonio faced. We see how that turned out."

"Tanji, I'm not your ex. To be honest, I don't want to hear his name no fucking more. I want you and I need you to put an end to all this crazy talk. I've officially been warned. We can't have kids naturally. There are other options. There ain't no more options on getting you. You're one of a kind. The kind I've been waiting for. I'm ready for the rest of my life and honestly, I envision it with you. Me, you, and Wright, the German Shepherd. Bet we have a life better than what that nigga could ever have. He lost it all when he lost you. I'm here now."

"Tavier—"

"T, stop fighting me and say you'll give me a chance to prove what I already know is true."

"When did you become so sure?"

"The moment your fine ass came home without a ring on your finger. I'm not passing up this opportunity to my happiness. Don't I deserve to be happy? You don't wanna steal it from me on Christmas. Don't be grinching my happily ever after."

I laughed as he took my hand. "I mean, I guess it wouldn't be the worst to find out."

"That's what I'm talking about. Now, let's go back and act like nothing happened. It'll drive my sisters crazy."

We headed back toward the house. "Did you tell them what happened the other night?"

"Yes and no. Cheyenne is the only one who got it out of me. Since she knows, the others might."

"Great." I rolled my eyes.

Two houses away from his parents', Tavier jumped in front of me. "Before we go in there, we have to make this official."

"Make what—" His lips shut mine up. The warmness of his tongue invaded my mouth. I sucked on his whiskey flavored tongue until mine tasted the same. Once I wrapped my arms around his neck, a moan escaped me.

Tavier pulled back. "Damn, girl. Hold up. Shit!"

"What's wrong?"

"You gotta chill on all that moaning. I can't go in here like this." He

looked down at his pants and what he referred to was hard to miss.

"Oh my...What you got in there?"

He laughed. "You gone find out soon."

"Who said I was easy?"

"Man, please. We grown. Relationships are the hard part. You getting this all up in you won't be."

I burst out laughing. "You are going to make this night hard."

"Shit. You already did. Let me fix this before we go in there." He stood between the cars in the driveway to hide his erection better. Once we got inside, he yelled. "Game time!"

CHAPTER NINE

WHAT THE HELL DID I JUST AGREE TO?

Tavier gave me nothing but trouble when no one paid attention. Licking his lips all slow right before biting the bottom one. Teasing me with every smile and chuckle.

I had to pull my damn hoodie off. It kept me nice and comfortable before Tavier got here. Now that sucker had me sweating like a heathen facing Jesus. My nerves were on edge too. Between his sisters and our parents, I had too many people watching my every move. Did they all listen to our conversation outside?

We played Pictionary first. Parents plus in-laws against kids plus Stephan. Things were awkward with him after all the talking we did earlier, but that quickly subsided. For Culture Tags, it was the women against the men.

The ladies tore the guys up, especially in the church and Black Twitter categories. Eventually, the kids moved into a bedroom upstairs because the older girls complained that we were too loud. We couldn't help it.

"Okay, we got this," my dad said, rolling his sleeves up. "Now, our women are killing us. We gotta get these."

The guys nodded and pumped each other up. It didn't work. Those Black Twitter cards killed them. Dad finally had one that he was way too confident about. The card had BCBC printed on it. Before my father dropped any hints, Tavier hopped up. "Big cock, big cum!"

The entire room went into an uproar. My dad threw the card down. "Boy, what the hell?"

"Have you lost your...damn mind?" Rhonda asked her son between laughs. She tried to catch her breath like the rest of us.

Terrell shook his head and dropped it in his palm. "That don't make no damn sense. That's your son," he told his wife.

Meanwhile, the younger men gave each other daps and gave this fool props for saying the worst thing possible. Once Tavier's eyes met mine, he winked.

"Y'all are just nasty," my momma said once we settled down.

"Yeah, but he ain't lying." Dad dipped his chin and winked at her. That started everyone up again.

"Ewww, Daddy!" I lowered my head in embarrassment.

"Hey! Hey! Sometimes you gotta put it on the table," he said, serving his Kevin Hart impression.

My cheeks burned and my eyes watered. I hadn't laughed this hard in years.

After another two hours, it was after midnight and all the kids were asleep. The Wrights had a tradition of the grandkids spending the night with the grandparents to give the parents time to prepare and assemble gifts. Then everything would surround the tree by the time the kids woke up. It really made the holiday magical for them.

We helped clean our mess before leaving the house. My parents and I would return tomorrow afternoon for dinner and more games, hopefully with no crazy outbursts on Jesus' birthday.

Tavier was on my heels and walked me outside while everyone else said their goodbyes. "So, you wanna come over to my place and sit on Black Santa's lap?" He closed the door behind us.

"No, fool! I came here with my parents and I'm leaving with them."

"You've been such a nice girl. Black Santa wants to see you get a little naughty." Tavier pressed himself against me from behind.

I pulled away and faced him. "As tempting as that sounds, you gotta wine and dine me first, playa. Getting me wet does not automatically get you in my panties."

"Mmm. So, you admit I get you wet. Are you wet right now? Let me see." He pulled me into him again.

The door opened and scared the both of us. Tavier grabbed my wrists and held them up. "I told you no, Tanji. You can't have my goodies. I'm a respectable man." He looked over his shoulder in all of his horrible acting. "Ohh! I didn't see you guys there. I think you should get your daughter home. She's getting a bit handsy." He smirked.

Neither of my parents bought it. They knew better.

"Oh, I got your handsy." I pulled my hands from his to hit him.

"Do you see what I mean?" He failed to keep a straight face. "Can't stop touching me."

"Boy, get out the way." Momma passed through us and pursed her lips when we made eye contact. "Mmmhmm."

They reached the car and we were alone again. "Goodnight, stupid."

"Goodnight, sexy."

Momma gave me the business the entire ride home.

Both of my parents did. They took me down the hypothetical lane of Tavier and I hitting it off. Once they mentioned grandkids, I zoned out—another set of people who'd eventually be disappointed once reality settled in.

Dad made his traditional Christmas morning gingerbread pancakes for breakfast. I had missed out on this the last few years. After breakfast, we chilled in the living room and opened our gifts. Momma handed me an envelope.

"This came in the mail yesterday. I figured it was a Christmas card."

"From who?" I asked. She shrugged.

It had a St. Louis address, but no name. I assumed it was from one of my friends up there.

Momma opened the new charm I got her and hugged me. The moment I opened the envelope, Antonio's face appeared. I pushed that sucker back in.

"Who was it from?" Momma asked. "People back in St. Louis."

"Aww, that's nice." She smiled, handing me a gift.

I ripped the paper off, imagining it being Antonio's face. He was always on some bullshit. Especially since the divorce. "Oh, my goodness, Momma! This is beautiful! Thank you!" I hugged her for my decked out journal.

Momma had introduced journaling to me, which helped me through so much. It inspired me to start my business. This one was personalized with my name and pictures of me on the cover. She must've searched through all the photo albums from my childhood for these pictures. She even wrote the first entry.

"Oh, uh-uhn. You are not about to have me snotting and crying this morning. I'm reading this when I'm alone. You always find a way to make me break down into tears."

She bounced her shoulders. "The truth cleanses you like that sometimes."

"Mmmhmm. So, when are we heading to Rhonda's?"

"Maybe around four."

"Oh, good. That gives me time to sleep the rest of that liquor off."

"Girl, you preaching to the choir. You know they're going for round two. That whole family drinks like fish. It does nothing to them. I'm telling you; they are not normal. Rhonda and Terrell always drink us under the table. We've learned to stay in our lane."

I took my gifts to my room and threw myself onto my bed. The Christmas card fell onto the floor. I should have thrown it in the trash, but I was too weak to get it.

My eyes shut for what felt like a few minutes. Momma knocked on the door. "We're leaving in an hour, Tanji."

I hopped up. "What?" I grabbed my phone and saw that I had slept for over four hours. How?

Tavier texted and called me this morning. I returned all the missed Merry Christmas texts before getting ready to shower. I cleaned up what had fallen off my bed, including the stupid card from Antonio. Against my better judgment, I pulled the card all the way out and my chest tightened.

This asshole had really sent me a family photo of him, that woman, and the baby. Who the fuck did that?

Like an idiot, I flipped it open and immediately regretted it. His handwritten note made me sick to my stomach.

The best gift you ever gave me was walking away gracefully. All I wanted was a real woman who could give me the family I deserved. Too bad you couldn't give that to me. I hope you can have a decent life even though you can never have this.

Antonio "Finally a Father" Simmons

I must've read it ten times, letting each time pierce me

deeper than the last. My teardrop hitting the ink and smearing it finally pulled me away from it. I dropped the card in the trashcan and got in the shower.

CHAPTER TEN

I'D BEEN DEALING WITH MY FAMILY FOR HOURS, waiting patiently for my baby to get here. She hadn't answered my last few texts. I wanted to make sure she wasn't having second thoughts on what we'd talked about.

The front door opened and I damn near broke my neck looking for her. It was my brother-in-law Greg. Damn.

"You in love already?" Mom popped my shoulder. She lowered herself onto the couch next to me with a slice of pecan pie.

I sucked my teeth. "Come on now. You know me better than that."

"Exactly, I already know the answer to my question." She bumped my knee with hers. "All I can say is you better not screw it up with her, boy. Tanji done been through enough with that damn idiot she married all them years. She don't need you playing no damn games. You hear me?"

"This is me! Why you think—"

"Tavier, I've seen all them females you've had all up in my house over the years. You haven't been even an ounce serious about any of them. Well, except that last one. I told you something was wrong with that girl." Mom rolled her eyes, remembering Lauren. I wouldn't say we were serious, although it was the longest relationship I had in a long ass time.

"This, my son, is another level. Tanji got your nose so open, a breeze will have your ass taking flight." She cackled at her corny ass joke. "All I'm saying is that you can't act like you did with them other girls. If you want to be serious, show it in your actions. I'm telling you; it'll only take one time for a woman like Tanji to chuck up the deuces on yo' ass."

"God, you're so old." I chuckled as she elbowed me. "I hear you though. I got this."

"Sure you do."

"Ay, let me have a bite."

She fed me a piece of her pie. "Don't ask for no more."

"Hey, hey! Merry Christmas!" Ms. Octavia said as she opened the door. I stared her way until I laid my eyes on Tanji. Something was wrong.

Tanji put some food containers on the counter without speaking to anyone. Then she walked back out. I greeted her parents before racing outside to make sure she wasn't leaving. I caught her at the trunk of her mom's truck.

I held her from behind. She wriggled her way from my embrace. "I'm not in the mood right now, Tavier."

"Not in the mood for what? I'm only hugging you."

"I don't want to be touched."

I examined her face and spotted the light redness in her eyes. Who had her crying?

Tanji closed the trunk after removing three bags of wrapped gifts. I reached for them. "Tavier, please leave me alone. I don't need your help," she yelled.

I jumped in front of her. "I didn't ask if you needed it. I'm giving it to you, anyway. You need to chill with that attitude. Everybody is having a good time. Whatever you got going on, leave it at the door. I'll talk to you when you calm the hell down." I kissed the corner of her mouth and left her standing there.

When I put the gifts by the tree, I took my ass in the kitchen to get some pie. Whatever was going on with Tanji would not get fixed until she wanted it to.

Tanji finally joined all of us as we filled our bellies with the smoked turkey legs Dad had worked on all morning. The women tore it up with the sides. This second plate would knock me out later.

My sisters asked Tanji about looking like her world had just ended. She blamed it on not feeling well. They let her off the hook.

My nieces hadn't noticed the new gifts under the tree until we'd finished eating. The Bailys always got them something like another set of grandparents. It was Christmas morning all over again. The girls thanked them and gave Tanji hugs first. Her mouth trembled the entire time. What the hell was going on with her?

After the girls took their toys upstairs, Tanji headed for the door. Mr. Mason witnessed the same thing I did. Her tears. We both followed her. I beat him to the door and asked if he'd let me check on her. He smiled, giving me his blessing.

I found her at the truck again. Her legs dangled from the back. I pushed her leg over to sit next to her. "T, are you gonna tell anyone what's up or do we have to keep guessing?"

"I'm good." She kept her head down like she was hiding.

"I can see that. Most people cry and rush out the house on Christmas. Then hide in trunks, all because they're good. Yeah, that works."

Every time she started up again, her mouth twisted. She turned her head away. I lifted her chin to make her look directly at me. "Let me see you. I need to have this image burned into my memory, so I make sure to never allow it to happen again."

46

Tanji rolled her eyes, releasing the tears that welled up. She acted like wiping them fast meant they hadn't fallen. "I told yo' ass to leave me alone. This is not your problem, Tavier."

"Guess I'm as hardheaded as you. So, what's up with you? No bullshit either."

She leaned her head on the window. "I'm being stupid. Letting shit get to me. I realize I look crazy, but this shit hurts more than I prepared for."

"Your divorce?"

"I wish that was all I had to deal with. It's so much I'm tryna keep together but it's not working."

"Well, God gave me ears to listen and a shoulder for you to cry on. I mean, if you want it. You be acting funny."

She barely laughed. "I know I do."

I waved for her to come closer so I could hold her. She rested her head on my shoulder and poured out everything on her heart.

Hearing about some Christmas card from her ex had my blood boiling. I wanted to hop in my car, drive to St. Louis, and whoop his ass in front of his woman and baby. I never understood why men went out of their way to say wild shit to women they supposedly didn't want.

"Man, don't sweat that nigga. He will get everything he deserves in life, and so will you. Bet money that kid probably ain't even his."

She burst out laughing. Something I gladly welcomed. That shell she'd wore worn when she first arrived cracked a bit.

Tanji explained the experience of having four miscarriages with him. The last was from fertility treatments. Apparently, her ex rubbed it in her face about how much money he'd wasted on her. He spewed some off-the-wall shit to her, which explained a lot. Most of how she saw herself came from what he'd repeatedly said to her. It was now my job to help her break that habit.

CHAPTER ELEVEN

Tavier turned out to be more mature than I remembered. I was just fine moping and beating myself up today. Crazy as it sounded, I believed Antonio had a point. Not being able to have children made me feel less of a woman.

The one thing I always looked forward to became something I couldn't physically accomplish. It killed me. Seeing him get that from someone else after he basically kicked my ass to the curb made me accept that I deserved it. My momma had taught me better. She exemplified the options I had, but none of that was enough for Antonio. Our child had to have his blood and nothing less.

How did I let him get to me?

I was more pissed at myself for allowing his bullshit in. Tavier gave me precisely what I'd needed. My parents had no idea Antonio had sent that card. It brought up so many fears and deceitful affirmations that I was nothing.

Year after year, loss after loss, I heard so many variations of my dwindling worth in my ex-husbands eyes. Our marriage started off great before we learned the truth about my body's inabilities. At first, I trusted our love would carry us through. Until it didn't.

Tavier pretty much waltzed in as if he had been preserved for me. The moment we ran into each other in the grocery store, I came alive again. He made things light and almost weightless. I hadn't experienced such honesty with Antonio. At least not in a positive way.

When I got it all out, my tears had dried up and my face hurt from laughing. Tavier made the world make sense. He brought up the damn dog too. I needed this time with him. It almost seemed like he'd sensed it. Like he understood me.

I got a text from my dad, asking if I needed him. That was our cue to go back inside. I hopped out of the truck only to get pulled into Tavier's manhandling ass hug.

"I'm here for you, Tanji. You don't have to do any of this alone. Whenever you need me, I'ma be there. I might not say what you want, but I will give you what you need."

"How do you know what I need?" I leaned my head back to look up at him.

Tavier gently bit the corner of his mouth. "The same way you are what I need. No explanation required. It's the way it is."

"Mmm." I stood on the tips of my toes to savor the warmth of his lips on mine. "Guess I should accept it already, huh?"

"That's what I'm tryna tell yo' ass. Trust me. Trust us. You'll never want for anything again. Watch."

"I'm watching."

WE DIDN'T GET HOME UNTIL ALMOST TWO IN THE morning. I experienced a high so good that I wanted to break in my new journal. I'd forgotten that Momma had written in it. My eyes watered after only the first line.

Tanjela LaVette Baily, Never Forget Who You Are. Don't let any man define you by his ignorance of why you were created. God is the only one who can restore you. If He sees fit like I trust that He does, you will have all that your heart desires. You will create the next generation of this family. I know you will.

I hate to see you hurting. You know that I have been where you are. You coming into our lives was God's answer to our prayers. Trust me when I say this is not the end of the road for you. No matter how you get there, you will get there.

I remember the day Tameeka left you on our doorstep. She wrote her brother a note with your name and birth date. You were one week old. We never knew she was pregnant. I had just lost our third pregnancy a month prior. You know the story well enough to know that miracles happen to those who believe in them. I didn't give up. I don't want you to either.

Tanji, I want you to live your life and love every moment. Stop dwelling on the lies you've allowed yourself to believe. I will do everything in my power to make sure you know your worth. You are divinely created for so much more than we can even imagine. You are a mother, just as I am your mother. Love is the key. I love you as my daughter, which makes you mine. Always remember that.

I love you with all of my heart and spirit. You are the joy of my life still to this day. That will never change. I will tell you who you are every day until you take over and believe it too.

Merry Christmas, Tanji Bear

Love Mom

I didn't bother wiping my face when I knocked on my parents' bedroom door. Daddy said to come in. I jumped in their bed and held onto my mother until all the tears I had left came out. She held me tight the entire time without saying a word. She only kissed my forehead over and over. Daddy rubbed my back in silence.

While I laid there, I thanked God for my parents. Like Momma said, love was the key. Even knowing they didn't bring me into this world, the love between us told me something different. My dad would always be my dad, and my mom was my mom. Tameeka died when I was ten. I literally felt nothing when it happened. My connection wasn't to her. We had no clue who my biological father was. I didn't care to find out.

Once our eyes were dry, we watched my mom's favorite movie, Norbit. Daddy fell asleep halfway in, but we made it to the end before saying goodnight.

Tavier texted me when he made it home and wanted me to call him in the morning. He'd asked to pick me up for lunch. Maybe he'd be a part of the family I'd have one day. I fell asleep wondering how life could be with him.

CHAPTER TWELVE

Tanji wore a grin like a damn kid when we got in my car. Mr. Mason had the talk with me briefly and in front of the women. The gist of the one-sided conversation was if I broke Tanji's heart, he'd break my neck.

Mr. Mason claimed he'd explain to my family why he did it and would deal with them if they had a problem. I assured her father there wasn't a need for threats, but he insisted that I make sure he didn't have to follow through.

"Daddy only came at you like that because he didn't get a chance to scare Antonio. He believes that if he did, I wouldn't have been treated the way I was."

"Let me make sure to get your dad some grandiose ass gift as a thank you."

"For what, crazy?"

"Not scaring ol' dude straight. I hate that you went through all that shit, but if you hadn't, you wouldn't be here with me."

She blessed me with another smile. "Yeah, I guess you're right. All experiences matter when you're searching for the real thing. The good, the bad, the ugly, and the beautiful. That's how you know what's real and what isn't. I've dealt with the bad for far too long."

"Now, you about to get these goods."

Tanji's mouth flew open. "Damn, Tavier. Can we ever have a conversation without you referencing your little business?"

"Blasphemy. Ain't not a damn thing little about my business. You bout to find out today."

She burst out laughing. "No the hell I'm not. I wasn't talking about the size, you idiot."

"Whatever. You better put some respect on my business."

"If I hadn't felt it for myself already, I'd say you were going a little too hard on defending it."

"Nah, I just don't want no rumors started."

"Negro, ain't nobody in this damn car but us."

"Somebody is always listening."

Tanji dropped her hand in her palm. "I can't with you."

"Yes, the hell you can. You most definitely will." I winked at her. The bellows coming from Tanji always put a smile on my face. Seeing her happy did everything for me.

Once we got to my building, I parked in the garage and we walked to my favorite burger joint. Tanji had my ass cheesin' hard in these streets. Like Mom told me, this was on another level.

I'd had fun with many women in my adult life, but being with this woman didn't compare to any other. The shit was foreign to me because what I thought was any ounce of love before wasn't a damn thing like this.

With Tanji, I legit breathed for the first time. She had no clue how ready I was to finally have something real. I wanted it with her. Tanji worried too much about what she thought she didn't have to offer. The woman herself was exactly what I wanted. She was what I needed—a future. I saw all of it with her, including kids. We'd find a way and I sure as hell wouldn't leave her side like the last fool.

Tanji was sexy and gorgeous from every angle. Her smart ass mouth kept me laughing. I usually had the upper hand on popping off at the mouth, but she was right up there with me. There'd never be a dull moment with her. As fine as her exterior was, I loved her mind, heart, and even that big ass attitude.

After lunch, we headed back to my building. We talked about how I had to stay hidden in my apartment on her moving day in a few weeks. Our deal was for her to give me a heads-up whenever any of my relatives came over. We still tripped over the fact that we'd be neighbors.

Once we'd exited the elevator and turned the corner, a woman stood at my door. The moment she turned to face us, I recognized her.

"Come the fuck on." I exhaled and dragged my hand down my face. What now? "Lauren, what are you doing here?"

"So, this is who you choosing, Tavier? You told me you needed a break. You never said you were moving on. I'm here for answers."

Tanji's face tightened as she tried to pull her hand from mine, but I held on tighter. Ain't no way was I about to let this shit with Lauren knock us backward. "Hold on, babe."

"Babe?" Lauren narrowed her eyes at Tanji, then pointed her way. "You're the one hugged up with him in those Facebook lives last night."

I held my hand up. "Ay, don't say nothing to her." I pulled Tanji to my door and unlocked it. "Go inside and wait for me." Her brow raised. "Please?"

Tanji's eyes pierced through me like she was cursing me out in every language known to man. My ass was in trouble. I'd fix it as soon as I got inside.

After closing the door, I faced Lauren. "Of all the fucking days you could've shown up, it had to be today." I rubbed my eyes. "Why are you here, man? It's been four months since I saw you. We haven't talked at all in like three."

"That's because I was giving you time. You told me you cared about me, but you needed space. You made me believe we had something."

"How? You flaunted other men every chance you got. How did you believe anything besides us being over?"

"They were only to get your attention."

I crossed my arms. "So, you didn't fuck any of them?"

Lauren opened her mouth, then stopped the lie before it came out. "That's beside the point. You told me it was a break, not a breakup. Now you gotta another bitch in there—"

I raised my hands too fast because she flinched. "Watch yo' damn mouth, Lauren."

"Why? You're gonna fight me."

"Man, get outta here with that. I'm not tryna put my hands on you."

"That's not the way I remember it. You couldn't keep your hands off me." She stepped closer.

"And you couldn't keep yours off my wallet."

Her mouth dropped. "Is that why you're dumping me?"

"Is that why you fucked with me? You wanted what I could buy you. Don't stand there and lie about it being anything more."

"That is not true." I posted up again, tired of her bullshit. "Okay, maybe it was. But not anymore. I miss you. You can't possibly feel for her how you did for me. We were together for almost a year."

"You're right about that. I don't. With her, it's real. It's genuine. It's most likely forever. So, all this you're doing ain't necessary. I've given you enough of my time. I hope you have a good life but don't show up here no more."

"Are you serious?"

"Extremely." I opened the door just as Tanji pulled it. "Where you going?"

"My Uber is downstairs." She pushed me out of the way, heading for the elevator. "Y'all can have each other."

"Tell me you playing, Tanji." I followed behind her.

She didn't answer me. Lauren hadn't moved from my door. I wanted to slap the smirk off her face, but I didn't put my hands on women in that way. "Tanji, let me lock up. Do not get on this elevator without me." I jogged back to lock my apartment up. The last thing I needed was Lauren entering it unsupervised or at all, for that matter. By the time I made it to the elevator, the doors closed. "Fuck!"

I stood there, watching the numbers descend. The other elevator was too far away for me to catch her. Lauren tried to wrap her arms around me from behind. I knocked her hands off as soon as she touched me.

"Doesn't seem like paradise to me. Isn't that some sort of sign? I didn't know she'd be here with you. Your sisters' posts filled my notifications last night. Seeing you with someone else showed me that—"

"Let me stop you. The only sign here is that you need to mind your business. If you saw me with her, that's exactly what you should've concluded. I'm with her. No subliminal message. It's black and white. Please don't come back here." The elevator dinged, and the doors opened. "Let's go."

Her face lit up. "Where are we going?"

"I don't know where you're going, but it ain't with me."

"Asshole."

"Whatever." We rode the elevator down to the first floor without a word spoken. I was too busy texting Tanji since she ignored my calls.

On the way to her house, I called Mom to tell her what

happened. "Damn, you messed it up in less than twenty-four hours?" She cracked herself up. I desperately needed an interception. She came up with a plan and put it in motion.

CHAPTER THIRTEEN

Tanji

Momma called asking me to meet her and my dad at Rouxpour. I didn't want to nor did I want to explain why. I informed the driver of the destination change.

I leaned my head back, praying I'd hold it together. How stupid was I? Of course Tavier had other women. He looked the part and he talked a good game. This was precisely why I'd rather keep him as a friend.

My heart had had enough. I'd barely picked up the pieces from the last shattering. Putting it back together wasn't the most challenging part. Trusting anyone else to hold it was. Tavier almost had me.

After everything with my ex, the last thing I wanted to do was jump into a relationship. My initial plan to wait a couple of years went head-to-head with Tavier and flew out the window. All because he spoke the right words. I should kick my ass for falling for the bull so damn quick.

The driver pulled up to the restaurant. I paid her an extra tip for the detour. When my parents' faces remained unseen, I called my mom. She told me they were around the corner, so I waited at the bar with a bottle of water.

"You really gon' walk away from me that easily. And you think I'ma let you?"

I exhaled slowly before turning his way. "Please tell me you didn't have my momma lie for you, Tavier."

"You wouldn't have come otherwise."

I leaned forward on the bar in need of something to hold me up. "Where's your girl?"

"I'm looking at her."

I swung my head left and right, scanning the room. "Don't see her."

"Cute." He ordered a beer. "Why you run off like that? I asked you to wait on me."

"Oh, I did. You had me waiting too long."

"Man, I wasn't even out there five minutes."

"That's four minutes and fifty-nine seconds too fucking long, Tavier," I said louder than I wanted. I pulled cash from my wallet and dropped it on the bar before leaving his ass once again.

Less than a minute later, he found me on the side of the building, rushing to get another ride. He snatched my phone. "What's this really about?"

"You! Tavier! You and every other lying man I took this kind of shit from. I'm not doing it anymore. Whatever you want to label your women is your business. You don't owe me no explanations. Now, give me my phone so I can go home."

"So that's it? You're quitting on me before we even start?"

"Better now than later, when I'm too far gone to smell the bullshit. Been there, done that. I'm done."

"Man, I'ma need you to stop comparing me to whoever really got you in your feelings. I didn't do shit. Lauren caught us both by surprise. I told her what was up and sent her on her way."

"Yeah, okay. Next week it'll be somebody else. No, thank you."

"Damn, T. Do you ever listen to yourself? Or anybody else, for that matter? I hadn't seen her in months. She assumed she'd slide back in. I shut it down because I want you. I will not hurt you, Tanji." He stepped closer to me but got stiff-armed.

"You think you can just tell me how it is and be done with it?"

He bounced his shoulders. "When I'm telling you the truth. Yeah."

"How can you be so sure you won't hurt me? You damn near did it just now."

"Because I'm feeling that shit too. Hurting you kills me. I need you to be happy so we can be. For the first time in my life, my heart is threatened. I don't know what you did to me, but I don't want to do life without you from this point on. We haven't even made love and I'm already invested in this.

"Shit, you got me out here saying making love instead of fucking. I wasn't really sure I had a heart until you got on the elevator. No woman ever came close to even seeing it and here you are with it in the palm of your hands and you don't even realize it."

"What are you saying to me right now?"

"I'm saying I'm already in love with you. I want to marry your ass one day. I want to get some ugly ass dog for you to baby and get a big ass dog for your protection when I'm not around. I want it all with you."

"You keep saying all this good sounding stuff now. I'm telling you this is not what you want. All of this is too much. What do you want from me?"

"I don't want anything from you. I simply want you, period. All of you. I want your joy, your pain, your dreams, and your fears. I want you, Tanji."

"We can't all get what we want."

"True. However, I trust God to give me what I need. This

time around, my needs and my wants are the same. I need you."

As much as I fought to suck it up, tears rolled down my cheeks. I didn't want to believe him. "No one needs me. I can't give you what you will need in the future. I'm defective."

Tavier shut his eyes and stood still with his head hung low. Maybe he'd finally heard me. He pulled at his collar like he had to loosen it. After scratching the back of his neck, he finally looked at me again. "I'ma act like you did not just say that."

I shrugged and turned away from him. My mouth wouldn't stop trembling. I didn't want to break down about this again. "You know what's crazy? Fatima asked me why I keep avoiding coming to her house to hang out. You know why?" I faced him after drying my eyes.

He slid his hands into his front pockets and exhaled. "Why, Tanji?"

"I try so hard to be happy for other people. It's no one's fault that my body doesn't work right. It's not fair. I can't be around her or Cheyenne too much because all they do is talk about their kids. Kids that are the same ages as mine would've been. Fatima is pregnant with her fourth child. How many times was I denied? Four, Tavier.

"Then they complain about how hard it is when I will never have it. I can't hold a baby in my womb for more than eight weeks. That's all I get. You are from a big family and you will eventually want what everyone else has. I don't want to hold you back because I can't give you everything you deserve. I'd rather you leave me alone and find someone who can."

He shrugged as he inched his way closer to me. "I hear you and I understand you've been through a lot of pain and loss. In no way do I want to diminish what you feel because of it. But life has to go on. You have to see beyond that. What does your mom always say? Speak life and live."

"Speak death and die. The power of life and death lies in

our tongues." I laughed. "You remember that?"

"Man, our moms kept us in church. The habit hadn't left me. My mouth gets me into trouble, but it's all in fun." He shrugged. "Believe it or not, I trust God. I don't always know how He's gonna do things, but I know how to trust Him. Something my mom taught me and your mom taught you. Notice how I say your mom. Even with no blood relation, do you see Ms. Octavia as anything less?"

"No."

"Do you see her as defective?" He used air quotes with that one.

"No."

"Then help me understand how you think your life can't find the same joy hers did. The same I'm finding in my own life. You give that to people." Tavier reached for my hands. I placed them in his. "Listen to me. You are not defective, Tanji. You're not. I don't want you to say that shit again."

I laughed. "Oh, we're back to cussin'. Where'd Pastor Wright go?"

Tavier smiled with his eyes. "He makes his appearances. Not for long, though. I keep him locked away to keep me in check. Seemed like you needed him for a few minutes."

"Seems so."

"Tanji, let me make something very clear. So clear that I'ma need you to accept it when I tell you this. I don't give a damn if you can't have kids. I'm in love with you, Tanji. Do not say it back 'cause I already sound all weak and vulnerable and shit. You do that to me."

I laughed in his face. He proved again that he wasn't at all what I was used to. Maybe that scared me more than his ex waiting at his door or his acceptance of what I offered.

Tavier operated in unknown territory. Transparency and honesty. Even with his own foreign emotions, he had no issue saying them out loud. I'd never seen that before.

CHAPTER FOURTEEN

 *Tavier*

Back at my condo, the moment I locked the
door, I grabbed Tanji's hand to close the gap between us. She
lost her balance, crashing into my body. To keep her from falling, I held onto her ass with a hand on each cheek. When she
didn't contest, I served her my tongue, hoping I'd finally get to
taste her. It had been on my mind the day I'd seen her in the
grocery store almost a month ago.

Moments later, I lifted her shirt. She pushed my hands off
of her. "No. We can't."

"We can't what? Don't do this back-and-forth shit with
me right now, T. Come on."

"I told you, Tavier. You have to wine and dine me first."
She smirked before glaring at me like she'd challenge anything
I had to say.

"How about I pour you a glass of wine then I dine on
you?"

"Boy, shut up. We have to take it slow."

"Slow?" I could work with slow. Placing my hands on her
arms, I pulled her closer. "A'ight, I promise you I will slowly

run my tongue all over your body and when I reach your sweet spot, you will yell for me not to stop."

Tanji shivered in my arms. "Do not say stuff like that, Tavier. You're gonna have to work for all this." She motioned her hand over her body as she walked away and found a spot on my couch.

I went to the kitchen to get on that wine for her. If she only knew that I already made accommodations for her. All of this was supposed to go down after lunch.

Before I picked her up earlier, I bought six different bottles of wine. There were too many to take a guess, so now she had choices. I didn't do wine and sure as hell didn't stock up on it for no one.

Tanji had my ass doing the most. "You staying here tonight 'cause I'm exhausted as fuck, chasing after yo' ass."

"You didn't have to."

I handed her a glass of red wine the liquor store lady assumed she'd like. "And not have you with me right now?"

She took a sip. "Mmm. This is good."

"You're welcome."

"I didn't say thank you."

"You should have. Mean ass." I lowered myself onto the couch next to her with a glass of Hennessey.

"I'm not mean. I just don't want to get sucked in."

"Something needs to get sucked on in this muthafucka."

Tanji gasped and put her glass on the coffee table. I got hit a few times in the chest. "You bastard. That is not how you get anything sucked, sir."

"I was talking about my mouth, your breasts. I'm down if you tryna go down, though."

She bent over laughing. "I cannot with you, boy. You just had to ruin it."

"Man, whatever." I set my glass down and picked hers up to hand to her.

She leaned back on the couch after another sip. I lifted her legs and rested them across mine. I removed her shoes, then massaged her feet. "Mmm. I needed this."

"Yeah, I could tell. It was a long day for the both of us."

"Oh, please. Having a beautiful woman waiting at your door is probably a regular thing for you."

"Not at all. Today was the scariest day I've experienced in a long time, though."

"Damn, what did she do?"

"Not her. You." Tanji focused on my face like she was reading me. "I thought you wouldn't believe me. The way you took off, I feared you left me for good. You scared the hell out of me. Losing you before you realize what I already know felt like weights on my chest, making it hard to breathe. That shit never happened to me and I swear I didn't know what I'd do if you hadn't trusted me."

"Tavier, I'm sorry." She rolled her eyes and exhaled. "When I saw her, I saw Antonio and his woman. It brought back the many conversations I gave them privacy to have because he'd lied about the content. Everything was about work with him that last year. She definitely popped up at our house a few times. He acted like it was a work emergency and made me wait inside."

"Shit."

"Yeah, it was some shit. I realized we weren't in the best place after everything, but I still trusted him. Seeing that woman today and you sending me inside took me back to a place I promised myself I wouldn't allow myself to be again."

"I didn't know, babe." I gently squeezed her ankle.

"How could you? So, I'm sorry for scaring you. It scared me too. Especially since it's you."

"Whatchu mean?"

Tanji lifted her eyes to the ceiling for a few moments. "You are..." Tanji bit her lip and focused her brown eyes on mine.

"You are nothing like anyone I've been with. I already trust you, and I don't like how that feels. Letting you in so easily can lead me down a different path but similar ending as the previous one. And I really like you. As a person, I like you. I don't want to lose you if we do this thing full out and it doesn't work. On the other hand, it's like I'm not giving my life a real chance at happiness if I don't see what we can be."

"Shiiit. We can get married right now today."

"Boy, shut up."

"Nah, for real. I don't want to date you, Tanji. That's the learning process. I know you. Most of you. The darker parts that you keep in will take time until you want to share that. But every other part of you I am already in love with. We don't have to do what everybody else does. We don't have to wait unless you truly want to. I'm just telling you it's a done deal for me. Nothing you can do will make me turn my back on you. I for damn sure will not hurt you. I'm ready to shop for puppies and shit. Let's do this."

"You stupid."

She put the empty glass down. "You're done with the wine. Can I dine now?"

Tanji pursed her lips. "I am kinda hungry. What do you want to eat?"

"Don't ask me that shit. I already told you the answer."

"What are you—" I yanked her legs my way so her body would fall in line. In a few movements, I had her straddling me. "Tavier," she whined.

"Tanji." I rested my forehead on hers, taking her all in. Her scent filled my nose. Her slow breaths matched mine. She got comfortable on my lap and stopped fighting me. "I need you, baby."

"I need you too," she whispered back.

I leaned in closer to her lips to see how far she'd go. The

moment our lips connected, I sensed she'd let me have her. That was my cue to keep my mouth shut. I had a habit of making her hesitate. Neither of us needed that shit tonight.

Slipping her my tongue, I slid my hands under her shirt with no contest. Feeling her skin made my dick hurt. It was too restricted and pissed at me for not getting it wet yet. I sucked it up as I suckled her tongue. Tanji's soft moans had my shit throbbing.

I scooted to the end of the couch to lift us. Tanji wrapped her legs securely around my waist as I made my way to my bedroom. Our mouths never released from one another.

After gently laying her across my bed, I stood over her. This woman was so fucking sexy with her low lids watching me as I kept her waiting. Tanji fucking Baily was in my bed. I'd had many women in my life, more for only one thing. Witnessing a woman holding my future in her palm did something different to me. I had something to prove.

I stripped naked before touching her and she watched me drop every piece of clothing with hungry eyes. Her brow raised when she finally saw the tool that was going to seal the deal tonight.

I peeled her jeans and panties off of her to reveal the meal I'd been waiting on. "Mmm. You are so fucking gorgeous, babe. Damn." That was all mine, even if I was the only one who realized it now.

Hovering over her, our eyes met, and she took me in. This woman made me understand things I hadn't before. This was what my parents kept getting on me to find. All this time, it was with Tanji. I savored her tongue once again, then I pressed my lips on her chin down to her neck. "Do you have a condom? It's not that I don't trust you, but you got that hoe vibe and I ain't tryna get no STD."

I laughed into her neck. "You are a fool, girl. Yes, I have

condoms. Don't touch a woman without one. Now, shut up and let me do what I does."

I unbuttoned her shirt, then unsnapped her bra from the front. She pulled everything off and tossed her clothes on the floor.

I took her nipple into my mouth as I caressed her other breast. Biting her caused her body to shudder beneath me. The warmth of my body rushed to one spot when she took my dick in her hand. My head dropped as she began stroking my shit. "Mmm."

"You better not break my coochie with that thing, Tavier."

"I got you."

"No, I got you," she corrected me as she sped up her movement.

"Shit."

"Tavier?"

"Yeah, baby?"

"I think I love you too." The moment she said those words, I froze. Lost in her eyes, she broke the brief silence after palming my scrotum. "Let me taste you first."

Tanji was fucking up my plan, but I didn't fight her since she literally had me by the balls. We switched positions without her releasing me, even for a second. Her steady pace threatened my concentration. Wasn't no way I was about to cum before she did.

Once Tanji tongued the head of my dick, I grabbed her by the waist and flipped her ass around until my feast hovered inches from my face. I couldn't wait to lap my tongue in her essence and dove right in. She moaned as my mouth covered her pussy. I folded my tongue to enter her, making her arch her back.

"Oh, my god, Tavier."

I held her waist with one arm and slapped her ass with the other. Finding her pearl was the simple part. Me holding her in place was a challenge. She kept trying to run away from me and I wasn't having that.

I tugged on that small round bean that drove her crazy. It was sensitive because I barely touched it and her loud moans bounced off the walls. For minutes I got a full serving of my baby's natural essence as she came back-to-back in my mouth. I didn't let up either. This time around, I slid two fingers inside of her.

The tightness had my dick ready to be just as snug when I finished.

She maneuvered her way from my grasp that had kept her in place this whole time. "Gotdamn you, Tavier," her voice rasped, showing me I had done my job right.

"Told you I was hungry."

"So am I." That was the last thing I heard before she covered my dick with the warmth of her mouth.

"Oh, shit."

Tanji must've been fronting on my ass earlier because she damn near devoured my entire shaft. There wasn't a damn thing I could do but grab at the air. She reached up and rubbed over my chest and abs. With no hands, she took me like a fucking pro.

"Mmm, shit girl. Fuck." Hearing her slurp as she pulled up, covering only my head had my fucking toes looking like I had arthritis. I shook my foot to keep the sensation at bay, but dammit, that shit didn't work. Tanji bobbed her head slowly until she took as much as she could fit in her mouth. Then she sped up the pace and went back to massaging my balls. That was the last ounce of restraint I had. I held onto her head to keep her in place as I busted a big ass nut.

"What the fuck, Tanji? We picking out a ring tomorrow. Hell, naw."

"Shut up."

I pulled a condom from my nightstand. Before I could rip the wrapper open, she took it from me. "I trust you."

"You sure."

"It's not like you can get me pregnant. I want to feel you all the way."

She bit the corner of her lip and nodded. I was about to ask her again, however having her with nothing between us won the mental battle. I pushed her on her back and spread her legs wide enough for me to get between.

The moment I found her opening and sank into her, the shit was over. The audible wetness after a few strokes had me intoxicated. I closed my eyes and dug deep into her as she filled the room with screams every time I thrust into her love. She weakly punched me in the chest. I'd forgotten to ease into her like I'd usually do. It was too late to go back. I slowed my pace to give her time to acclimate to me.

"What the fuck, Tavier?" Her words dragged like she was just as drugged as I was. Every dip into her felt like she was trapping me. The pain in her squints each time I dug in hinted that I'd wait until next time to do all the things I wanted to. We'd stick to this position for now.

Tanji screamed and tightened her thighs around me for the third time. The restfulness on her face allowed me the gratification to let go of what I'd been holding onto. I pounded into her, causing her to scream louder than before.

The moment we caught our breath, I pulled out and got us towels. "You're gonna have to change your sheets. You let out a lot in me."

"Shit, what did you expect? Do you even know how it feels inside of you?"

She dropped her head back and laughed. "I guess. Now, I'm too tired to eat actual food."

"Yeah, you wore my ass out too."

"We going for round two once I take a nap."

"Shiiiit. You better hope I don't go into a coma."

"Shut up, stupid."

I got back in the bed with her. Minutes later, her breathing became slow and heavy. I watched her until my eyes were heavy. The fact that she had walked into my life right at the moment I prayed about finding a wife sent a chill up my spine. Tanji really was the answer to my prayers.

CHAPTER FIFTEEN

MOMMA CAME WITH ME THIS MORNING TO GET THE keys to my new place. When I came back to Houston, I only brought my belongings. That meant clothes, shoes, jewelry, almost everything in the kitchen except the utensils.

My Crockpot, cast iron pan, the toaster, coffee machine, blender, and even all of my spices came with me. I stripped the kitchen down because that was where I spent a lot of time making our meals. I'd be damned if another woman came in and used all of my hand-picked essentials.

Antonio sent me a pissed off text when he'd come home from work and I had already hit the road with my little U-Haul hitched to my Acadia. He'd gotten a dose of his own medicine.

To make it sting a bit more, I poured powdered bleach in the laundry detergent powder. I usually used liquid, but it was my way of getting back at him. I also put liquid bleach in the fabric softener. The man never did laundry. He wouldn't recognize the difference. Lord, did it make me laugh until my ribs hurt when he'd sent me pictures of his clothes with bleach stains. I suggested that he did something wrong and left it at that.

I threw away all the pictures and left the wall decor because I didn't want any reminders of the house I'd shared with that idiot. I would've left my pots and pans, but I wasn't about to repurchase all of that when we had everything I needed for my kitchen.

Momma and I spent all last week furniture shopping and scheduled the deliveries for today. My bedroom, dining room, and living room sets had arrived an hour ago. Rhonda had invited herself over to help me decorate the place after I went on and on about her style. It was very similar to mine. I welcomed the help from a pro.

Momma helped me put most of the groceries away. We took a quick trip, so I'd have something to cook for the week plus some snacks for right now. We cleaned the apartment down before the furniture came and worked up an appetite.

After buying groceries, I reminded her about hitting the town with me. She wanted to wait for my dad, so we'd go together. My dad and Tavier had agreed to help me move the storage room stuff when they got off from work.

"How's business going?" Momma asked as she sat at my new table.

I continued stocking my spice cabinet. "It's fantastic! Everything is flowing so much better since I hired a VA and freelancers. Both websites are making so much more since I'm not doing it alone."

Momma scoffed. "See what happens when you finally listen to your mother? I told you that when you only had one store. That was a lot of work even then."

"You were right, like always. I only wanted full control."

"That had you stressed out on top of all you were juggling. Now, I hope you can get back to candle-making. I need my

Black Beauty candles in my life again. You are so talented and I only want you happy with what you do."

"Trust me, that is exactly the plan. This summer to be exact."

"Ooh, I can't wait. I will be here to help with whatever you need."

I created simple journals for Black women with animated images I doodled. It started as a hobby, but my passion grew as the popularity increased. Social media wasn't my cup of tea, yet I did pretty good with my Etsy shop. That grew into stickers, pins, bookmarks, and a few print on demand products like hoodies and mugs.

When I'd begun this side business, it was only something to do to keep myself from spiraling. I drew images of what I'd thought my daughter would resemble. I'd imagined her with beautiful bronze skin, big curly hair, and big brown eyes. She was absolutely gorgeous. A suggestion from Momma to slap her on the cover of a notebook had turned into a full-fledged business.

My job as a sonographer for an OB-GYN damn near killed my spirit after we'd lost the second baby. I had to smile through it because I loved my job. I loved the idea of creating life and had started this career to experience the energy of excited, expectant mothers.

Once learning I couldn't make it beyond the first trimester, something had to take my mind off of my reality. I wasn't a graphic designer, but I had enough skill to create products with my drawings. At times, I'd tried my hand at whatever had the potential to make me happy. I had a candle phase that had left some unhappy customers when I'd lost pregnancy number three. That one took me through a slump and everything fell to the side. I shut it all down.

Antonio pushed for the fertility treatment. I opposed the idea because I didn't want the disappointment. He either had more faith than I did or was just desperate. Honestly, at that point, I was numb. The easy part was temporarily suppressing my emotions because I did it for a living with patients at the clinic. Only Shanice had witnessed my lows. She was a nurse at the same clinic and kept me going when nothing else worked.

Shanice listened to me, let me cry, let me say all the horrible things I'd needed to say. Then she'd pray with me. Somehow, she became my therapist in a way. We did so much together. Especially after Antonio claimed he'd had to work all those weekends after I lost our fourth pregnancy. He'd tell me he had to work so hard because of the treatment's wasted cost.

I held onto so much shit and helping other women see themselves through the characters I created for the journals helped me too. After taking a leave from work for mental health, I went back sort of refreshed. Months later, I complained about Antonio not touching me or talking to me like he used to. There were so many signs in hindsight. He didn't really hide what he was doing but being so locked into making sure I didn't have a mental breakdown distracted me.

The divorce papers hadn't surprised me as much as they'd hurt me. I'd thought we'd be able to come to terms with the cards we were dealt as husband and wife. He'd meant what he said about trusting that he'd have a baby with his blood. He never mentioned that he'd planned to get it from someone else.

When I moved back home, I ran my business full-time. Going back to a clinic would not work for me. My parents would've let me live with them forever. With enough savings to hold me for a while and thriving stores, this new career allowed creative freedom and time to scale up. I had a lot to give, especially after life halted those plans temporarily. This new year had begun better than the last ten. I only had one person to thank for that.

Tavier Adonis Wright's love held me tighter than any love

I'd ever received. In a short time, he'd shut out the negative affirmations I regularly spoke to myself. He reminded me I was enough. Hearing it from my parents helped, although you'd expect that from your parents. He had no reason to enter my self-hating bubble, destroying it from the inside. In less than two months, that man had helped me restore what the last decade had destroyed.

I had to accept that my original vision didn't have to be the only one. It could change. It had changed. Tavier forced me to realize the beginning of my story happened for a reason. Not having a child of my own didn't mean I couldn't have a child. It didn't mean I'd never have a family of my own.

Breaking the habit of being hard on myself was still a struggle. Tavier took it upon himself to wake me up with affirmations. Ones about me being destined and divine. If we didn't wake up together, he'd text me a message to remind me I was more than enough for him and for this life God gave me.

"Your dad is on his way. Is Tavier coming to help?"

"Mmhm." I read my watch for the time. "He should be here in about an hour. Then we'll all head to the storage unit. We should be able to pack all our cars with boxes. That's three SUVs and one sedan. It should work in one trip."

Momma smiled ear-to-ear. "So, when's the wedding?"

"What?" I failed to not cheese like she did. Tavier was a breath of fresh air that I now needed to make it through the day.

"Oh, girl. I see the way you look when you talk about that man."

"Momma, we barely made it official a few weeks ago."

"And? Love is love. You two are neck-deep in it."

If I was a few shades lighter, I'd have some rosy ass cheeks. My mother spoke the truth. But marrying him this soon was not the plan. She'd have to give us some time for that.

"I won't lie, I did sorta fall in love with him, which is weird. It's so soon."

"You've known him all your life. It's not like he's a stranger off the streets. You know what kind of man he is and that he comes from a wonderful family."

"I guess so. It was just unexpected."

"Love usually is. Mason was not my type in the slightest when we met. I actually liked his friend."

"What? You never told me that."

Momma nodded with a smirk on her face. "Your dad was always handsome. All the girls were crazy about him. He tried to talk to me at this party in high school. I turned him down flat out in front of everyone. He was so conceited and thought he could get any girl he wanted. Well, I showed him."

"How did that turn into thirty-six years of marriage?"

"He didn't take no for an answer. For months, he persisted with gifts. Little stuff. Candy, cards, single roses. We were kids. For a seventeen-year-old to be that sure of himself, I gave him one date. My goal was to shut him down again privately. I told him I didn't appreciate him doing all he did all because I told him no. That word was foreign to your dad. All the girls said yes. Not me. When he articulated that he'd tried for years to say nothing to me because he knew I was too good for him, he caught my attention."

"Too good, huh?"

"Oh, I was a good girl. I did my work and mostly stayed to myself. Your father told me he wanted to ask me out the first day he laid eyes on me four years prior. When I tell you that man explained the exact day down to the outfit I wore, he had me. For him to have paid that close attention and remember it all those years later, I knew he would be that attentive as a boyfriend. God knows he was all that and more."

"Aww! I love that."

"I see how Tavier looks at you. The way he handles you and your heart, he's the one."

"Momma, I promise you I feel the same way. It's scary though. I see us old together with a couple of kids. Adopted, of course. I want a life with him. After giving him so much push back, he saw through my barrier. Just that fast, he broke that sucker down."

"I'm so excited for you, Bear. You need a man like him. Someone who will uplift you. Someone who sees you even when you can't bear to look at yourself."

"Wow. That's exactly it. He sees me. Tavier helped me see myself again. Not the broken woman, but the strong one you taught me to be. I'm in love with myself again. I don't focus on what I feel I cannot do anymore. He reminded me of my worth and that's a gift I could never repay him for."

She pursed her lips and narrowed her eyes. "There are ways."

"Ew, Momma."

"Girl, hush. You pay him by putting it on that man so good, he can't even see straight."

"Ma!"

"I didn't make it to thirty-six years without learning a trick or twenty."

"If you try to show me anything that you do to my daddy, I'm gonna scream."

"Girl, I be having him screaming."

"Bye, Momma. I don't even need your help no more. You are banned from my apartment."

"Ugh, fine. I'll keep it to myself. But when you need to know some secrets, I'll put you on."

"I'm about to put in some ear plugs." We laughed. "I'ma tell him you said he screams."

"Do that and I will whoop your tail. Your booty meat will be sore until your kids are grown."

When someone knocked on the door, we immediately stopped laughing. Momma opened it and we made eye contact after my dad walked in. We burst out laughing at the same time. Daddy ignored us on his way to the fridge for water.

I hinted that I had something to tell him a couple times, but Momma cut me off each time. I let her make it only because Daddy might get embarrassed. Momma was lucky.

CHAPTER SIXTEEN

I OPENED MY EYES TO FILL MY VISION WITH THE perfect sight of beauty. Tanji talked a lot of shit. She was tough as hell to get through to. The same woman slept so peacefully next to me.

After using the bathroom, I wrote her a note and stuck it on the bathroom mirror. I tip-toed out of my bedroom to make her breakfast. The bacon and sausage fried in the same pan while I sauteed mushrooms and spinach in another one.

The aroma of the meat frying would wake me from the dead. I'd expected nothing less when she sauntered down the hallway toward me.

"Good morning, gorgeous."

Tanji's smiled put the sun to shame. Nothing naturally lit up a room faster than the corners of her mouth turning upward. She met me near the stove and planted those soft lips on me.

"It's smells so good, babe." She stole a mushroom. "Thank you for the note. I love waking up to this. You need me to do anything?" I shook my head and got another kiss before she sat at the bar.

"I'ma tell your ass now. This ain't about to be a habit of mine."

She giggled. "Why not? I love your omelets."

"Yeah, but you got me feeling all domestic and shit."

"Oh, so you think that women are the only ones who cook."

"Now, you know damn well that ain't what I'm saying. The way my mom had my ass in the kitchen with my sisters, she wouldn't let me ever believe that shit."

"I remember. She pulled me in a few times whenever I was at y'all's house. She used to tell you that all women can't cook and she didn't want you to starve if your wife couldn't."

We laughed at the memory. Mom had made sure I knew how to do everything for myself. "She was right, though. All women don't cook. Even the ones that try."

"Whatchu tryna say? I told you something was wrong with my stove."

"Man, I got the same appliances. You don't see me burning this food."

"Tavier, don't make me slap you. The maintenance people came and replaced the whole thing. If nothing was wrong, they wouldn't have done that."

"Man, whatever. Just remember that burnt and blackened ain't the same thing."

"Screw you."

"You already did that. Hence, the reason we eating breakfast so damn late. Can't keep your hands off me."

"You get on my nerves." She picked up her phone after it chirped. "Oooh, my mom is coming with your mom in a couple of hours."

"Isn't your housewarming tonight?"

"Yeah, but Rhonda really took to helping me decorate. Apparently they went shopping this morning and she found something for me."

"Again, she could drop it off at the housewarming like everybody else. Something is up. I know my mom."

"You think so?"

"Hell, yeah. Did you tell your mom about me living across from you?"

"Tavier, you asked me not to."

"That didn't answer my question."

"No, boy. Nobody ratted out Batman. Your secret is safe."

"Look, I'm lookin' out for the both of us."

"I'm sure it's not that bad. Plus, with me around, your mother will not pop up on you. She knows you'll be well taken care of."

"I got something for you to take care of after we eat."

"Dang, is that all you care about?"

"Fuck yeah, that's all I care about."

"Wowwww."

"Okay, not all the time. We're honeymooning, though. So, like I said, hell yeah."

"Do you see a ring on my finger?" She raised her hand in my face.

"It's invisible." I chuckled at her head-dropping cackle.

Damn, I loved her.

I fed Tanji only food this time. She made us some version of mimosas that had her tripping. Alcohol made her extra damn goofy if she started off in a good mood. Lately, that was all I witnessed. It was all I wanted.

Tanji put me on the allblk app, so we'd been watching nothing but Black movies any time the TV was on. We binge-watched *Monogamy* last week, which led to long-ass discussions about her darker moments. A character couldn't have children for different reasons than Tanji's, but it sparked up a lot for her. This time, we tried to keep the topic lighter.

We'd finished watching *Secret* before I needed another fix. Her time of the month had ended a few days ago and I missed being inside of her for that week. She'd have to oblige until I got it all out of my system. Honestly, that shit may never happen.

My baby straddled me like she had done the night before. All I craved was a repeat of her riding me like she was created to do it. Tanji had a nigga ready to give her anything she asked for, including the moon.

The moment I slid my hands into her panties, taking a handful of her bare ass, her phone rang. Tanji pulled back to get up.

I held her in place. "Let it ring, we'll only be a few minutes. You can call her back after."

"Tavier, stop playing. Let me make sure everything is okay."

Tanji jogged to the phone and answered it. I heard a woman outside on my way to the bathroom. It sounded like she was responding to everything Tanji said. I looked out the peephole and saw both of our moms in the hall.

Tanji met me at the door. "My mom is at my door."

"I know," I whispered. She continued to my room and put her clothes on. "Whatchu about to do?"

"Um, I'm going out there."

"My mom is here too."

"Okay, so, do you have a better plan? I just told her I was home. I can't lie and say I'm not."

"Shit, you did lie."

"Tavier, stop being a fucking child. Life will go on with your mom knowing where you stay."

"Dammit, T. I've been safe for five years. This is your fault."

"Boy, get outta my way."

Tanji made it past me to get her slippers by the front door. "Aye, tell them you were borrowing some sugar or some shit from a neighbor when you go out there."

"Uh, you can tell us yourself, Tavier," Mom said on the other side of the door.

I clasped my hands behind my neck. "Shit."

"Shit is right. Open this damn door, little boy." Mom knocked until I did as she said. When they walked inside, she popped me. "Go put on some damn clothes! Octavia is right behind me. Don't nobody wanna see you in your drawers." I stepped back into my room to throw on a shirt and shorts.

"Hi, Rhonda. Hi, Momma," I heard Tanji say.

"Hey my future daughter-in-law." Mom's tone was so much sweeter with Tanji.

The footsteps echoed down the hall to the living room. By the time I came out, my mom had her hands on her hips, checking the place out. "Very nice, son. Glad to finally see where you live. And right across from Tanji?"

"Yeah, that was a coincidence," Tanji responded to my mother.

"Looks like you have the same floor plan as Tanji. But without my touch, it's just as dull as expected. Mmmhmm." Mom shot her eyes at me. "Welp, now that I'm here. We need to get this place up to date, son. This is just ugly. Black is not the only color that exists."

"You already starting up. My house, my style. You can't touch anything. If you try to pop up on me, I will answer the door butt ass naked. So, don't try. Matter fact the both of us will." I motioned at Tanji.

Ms. Octavia burst out laughing. "Oh, my."

"No, we will not." Tanji nudged me. "He keeps saying this will be a problem, but it won't, right? I mean, we spend a lot of time together and I'd hate to get caught off guard like he fears we will."

"Tanji, you are about to be my daughter-in-law one of these days. I respect you and I love you. So, no. I will call and ask before I come over."

"What?" My mind was blown. Either she was lying or somebody had taken over my mom's body. "Me being with someone never stopped you before."

"Before you didn't have a woman in your life. You were hoeing around. How was I supposed to know what days you had them over?" She shrugged, all innocent like that was a good enough answer. "Tavier, I respect your privacy. Now that you officially have some business to mind with this lady right here, I will not interfere."

"I'll be damned. That's all it took?" I took my mom in my arms and squeezed her.

"Boy, let me go before you break something. It's date night and I need everything functioning for your daddy." I immediately released her and stepped away.

"You could've kept that last part to yourself."

All the women laughed. "Where's the fun in that? Good Lord, you should've had a housewarming, son. This really is awful."

They settled on one side of the couch while Tanji and I sat on the other. Our mothers literally planned out our lives with no word from us. For a few minutes, they told us when we should get married, when we should look into adoption, and even where we should look for houses once our leases were up. My baby leaned on me as we watched them.

"It's simply unbelievable for y'all to live next door to each other. We've been trying to figure out where this boy lived for years. The first place you get is right across the hall. That ain't nothing but God. When y'all were younger, I could have only dreamed of this boy finding a woman like you. With his hoeish ways, I didn't see it happening."

"Ma, chill on all the hoe stuff. I'm not about that life and I wasn't even a hoe. I simply enjoyed the benefits of being single."

Tanji lifted her head and faced me. "You miss those benefits?"

"Woman, please. I don't even remember what they are anymore. You erased every memory that didn't include you. My life hadn't started until you came into it."

Tanji mouthed, "I love you". I kissed her lips and almost forgot we weren't alone.

"Awww. How sweet?" Ms. Octavia said with the biggest smile.

"That's what I'm talking about, boy. He's just like his daddy. They always have the right words to say. Other times, they always say some stupid shit."

I dropped my head as we chuckled at my mother's mouth. If anything, stuff flew out of my mouth the same way it did hers.

Ms. Octavia pointed at me. "You'd better have a better answer to this question than my daughter."

I glanced at Tanji, who seemed as clueless as I was. "What question is that?"

Ms. Octavia leaned forward, looking me dead in my eyes. "When's the wedding?"

EPILOGUE

ONE YEAR LATER.

My natural alarm woke me up like clockwork. I could not hop up fast enough. For other people in my shoes, this was the toughest part. With all that I'd been through, I didn't dare complain.

When the second alarm when off, Tavier lifted his arm from his side of the bed. "I'll get him."

"Thank you, babe. I'll get her."

I waited for Tavier to walk over to my side of the bed, then joined him on the farthest side of the room. Tavier Jr. got his diaper changed first while I breastfed Talia. Once she finished, Tavier and I swapped babies and changed her diaper before walking out of the room.

"You want the works?" he asked me from the hall. I dropped my head. "Oh my gosh, yes!"

Saturday mornings had turned out to be the best day of my week. I had Tavier's help all day long. Throughout the week, I took care of the babies with my momma's extra set of hands.

Now that Momma had retired two months ago, she

treated us like her new job. Since the babies had arrived last month, she came over Monday through Friday. My mom really assumed the role of our nanny with no questions asked.

I still ran my business because of her. At first, I didn't see how I'd get anything done. Tavier told me to take a break from work, which wasn't a bad idea. I'd listened to him for the first month and a half. With print on demand products, my businesses ran themselves minus my weekly new arrivals.

The two freelancers I'd hired held up their end. Cheyenne and Shanice took care of doing cute product videos for Instagram and Facebook. Shanice had held it down in that department since last year. Besides Momma, she was my biggest fan and supporter.

My customers were more than understanding about me not putting anything new out right now. The candles were already sold out and had to wait until I had more time on my hands. I'd shared my personal struggles with my followers on social media and they were nothing less than supportive.

Popping out twins was nothing short of a miracle. All of my attention belonged to Talia and TJ. Those two angels gave my life a brand new meaning. The moment I accepted I'd become a mother, that was exactly what God did. You truly never knew what He had up His sleeve. We'd all received the surprise of a lifetime.

Tavier and I made sure to use protection most of the time since I hadn't wanted to become pregnant with his baby only to lose it. I loved him so much that I wanted to spare him of that heartache.

When I found out about my pregnancy only a couple months after we became a thing, I kept it to myself. Then my belly ratted me out because it poked out quicker than expected. I was a nervous wreck the entire time.

Once we made it halfway into the second trimester with a

perfect bill of health from my doctor, it hit me that this was really happening.

We'd rushed to the courthouse to get married. Tavier promised me a wedding with all the bells and whistles next year. I didn't even care about that. He was my husband, which was the whole point of a wedding—getting married. We did it with our family and had a little party in our building's ballroom.

The babies came the day after Christmas, surprising us all. We all thought we'd had another month left, even though my doctor warned me about the twins coming early.

We stood on pins and needles about them debuting on Christmas Day. Especially since I had gone into labor that night. Talia came out first at 3:14 a.m. and TJ arrived at 3:21 a.m. The gift of two perfectly healthy babies was the greatest present I'd ever gotten. Tavier's big ass had cried almost as much as I had.

Our place had boxes stacked up against every wall. Tavier moved into my apartment once his lease ended, so we'd put his things in storage. Tomorrow was our new moving day. I fought him on it because he'd swore Rhonda would overstay her welcome within the first week, but we bought a house fifteen minutes away from both of our parents' houses.

Today was our last day in this place. We'd spend the night at my parents' and the men would move everything in the morning.

I joined Tavier and Talia in the living room. He'd placed her into her bassinet while he cooked, so I put TJ in his right next to his sister. Every time I looked at them, my eyes watered. They were real and they were ours.

"Baby, what time are we leaving?" my husband asked me.

"Hopefully by three. I have to pack up the bathroom and the rest of the kitchen stuff."

"I can do that."

"Of course you can. Where were you the first time around, hubby? Could've saved me a lot of hard years and heartbreak."

"Probably somewhere being groomed for this very moment." He laughed at me rolling my eyes. "I told you, it's all in God's timing. Neither one of us were checking for each other back then. It had to work the way it did for us to see each other the way we do now."

"True." I bobbed my head. "That smells so good. Thank you for making breakfast."

"My ass gotta eat too. Besides, them babies of yours eat like they don't know how to do anything else. You need nutrients."

"Babe, they aren't even two months. All they can do is dirty their diapers and eat."

"When can they daddy eat something?" He rubbed his hands together and bit his lip. "I know damn well it's been six weeks, T."

"Barely. We have so much else to focus on right now. We'll have time for that."

"I want it right here and now." I hopped onto the counter after he plated the food. He handed me a plate but pulled back when I reached for it. "You can eat what you want when I can eat what I want."

"Oh my goodness, Tavier. Stop being childish. All that eating got us two babies at once." I looked back at them, resting peacefully. "God, I cannot believe we have babies."

"I can. You had to wait on me. Your body knew it. I hate that you had to experience all that you did, but look how it paid off."

"It's pretty amazing to go through something like that and then bam! Two babies at once."

"We need to get busy on the next bam!"

"No, thank you. I think two is enough."

"Fine." He finally gave me my food. "Still better feed me later."

"Or what?"

"Or I'm gon' walk around this bitch with my dick swangin' until you do. I don't care who sees either."

I almost fell off the counter with him pacing back and forth in the kitchen. He strutted like George Jefferson. I could only imagine him doing that naked. "You are crazy."

"Crazy about you. For sure crazy about the life you've given me."

I lowered my head and smiled. He had that effect on me. "Thank you, Tavier. For everything. We really hit the jackpot, huh?"

"Nah, the jackpot could never amount to this right here."

"I know that's right. This is priceless."

THE END

AFTERWORD

MERRY CHRISTMAS!!

Thank you so much for reading! I pray that you enjoyed the story. Tavier and Tanji were exciting to write. I think I'm enjoying friends-to-lovers stories these days lol.

Anyway, if you would, please leave a review about Tavier and Tanji. I'd love to hear (read) your thoughts on my first standalone Christmas story. Thank again for reading!

Bridgette & Telicia, I cannot publish any book without thanking you for your constant support. I don't even know how all of this would happen without having you two holding me down and sometimes holding me up when I feel like...well, y'all know! Love you both.

To the RAMs who took a chance on me, I wouldn't have the will to keep going this if y'all weren't on this journey with me. Y'all really stay on my mind whenever I get in front of my computer. I'm tryna impress y'all lol. I hope I have so far. Thank you for your support.

ABOUT THE AUTHOR

Renée is from the best city on the planet—Houston. She resides there with her three kids. She writes fiction based on African American characters. Renée loves creating stories with relationship drama that can easily be found in many households. She wants readers to see themselves or recognize someone they know in her characters. If she can make you laugh, gasp, think, or even cry, then her mission will be accomplished.

Connect with Renée: www.authorramoses.com
    On Facebook www.facebook.com/authorramoses
    On Instagram @reneeamoses
    On Twitter @authorramoses

Listen to Same Book, 3 Time Zones: A Book Review Podcast
    We read one book a month and post our discussion.
    www.sb3tzreviews.com
    On Instagram @sb3tz_reviews

Signup for latest news, first looks, and exclusive content: bit.ly/RAMList

ALSO BY RENÉE A. MOSES

Turns in Love Series
Two Lefts, One Right
Making a Hard Right
Straightaway
Wishing for Her (Christmas Short)
Truth Is...

Harris Sisters Series
The Cost of Loving You
I Thought I Knew You
Never Stopped Loving You
Not Good Enough For You

Standalone
You Could Do Damage
When the Time is Wright (Christmas Novella)*